Yuletide at Moonglow

YULETIDE AT MOONGLOW

A Moonglow Christmas Novella

DEBORAH GARNER

CRANBERRY COVE PRESS

Cranberry Cove Press / Published by arrangement with the author

Yuletide at Moonglow by Deborah Garner

Cranberry Cove Press
PO Box 1671
Jackson, WY 83001, United States

Library of Congress Catalog-in-Publication Data Available
Garner, Deborah
Yuletide at Moonglow / Deborah Garner—1st United States edition
1. Fiction 2. Woman Authors 3. Holidays

p. cm.
ISBN-13:
978-0-9969961-7-4 (paperback)
978-1-952140-06-8 (hardback)

Printed in the United States of America
10 9 8 7 6 5 4 3 2

For my mother,
who always made holidays special for us.

Books by Deborah Garner

The Paige MacKenzie Mystery Series

Above the Bridge
The Moonglow Café
Three Silver Doves
Hutchins Creek Cache
Crazy Fox Ranch

The Moonglow Christmas Novella Series

Mistletoe at Moonglow
Silver Bells at Moonglow
Gingerbread at Moonglow
Nutcracker Sweets at Moonglow
Snowfall at Moonglow
Yuletide at Moonglow

The Sadie Kramer Flair Series

A Flair for Chardonnay
A Flair for Drama
A Flair for Beignets
A Flair for Truffles
A Flair for Flip-Flops
A Flair for Goblins

Cranberry Bluff

ONE

Mist stood outside Timberton's candy store, watching the activity in the town square. The holidays always brought a sense of excitement and anticipation to the small Montana town, but this season surpassed that of prior years.

"It's so exciting, don't you think?" Betty said as she emerged from the candy shop. She took a place beside Mist and looked across the street.

Mist turned and smiled, not surprised to see a bag of caramels in Betty's hands. The homemade sweets were the hotelkeeper's favorite guilty pleasure. It was a rare day that a stash of the smooth, sugary treats couldn't be found in a drawer behind the counter of the Timberton Hotel's registration desk, not to mention a few in Betty's pocket.

"The tent is so big," Betty exclaimed, eyeing the large canvas structure surrounded by the trees and benches that graced the town plaza.

"Yes. Just as it will need to be." Mist pulled her wool cape closer as a chilly breeze kicked up. It was one of her favorite finds at Second Hand Sally's, the local thrift shop.

"They're expecting hundreds of people, possibly a thousand or more," Betty said. "Counting those coming in by shuttle from Helena."

"Delightful," Mist said. "The more the merrier, as the saying goes." It was true, as far as she was concerned. The Yuletide festival was a first for Timberton. It promised to be the event of the season, if not the whole year.

"We'll have a full house, that's for sure." Betty popped a caramel into her mouth and tucked the empty wrapper in her jacket's right pocket.

Mist nodded, thinking of the heavily noted pages in the hotel's reservation book. Not only would the regular yearly visitors all be back, but every room was booked.

"We're lucky two of the larger hotels in Helena decided to run festival packages," Betty said, as if reading Mist's thoughts. "We never could have provided rooms for everyone."

"Yes," Mist said. "And it will keep people safe on the way back at the end of the night since the hotels are running shuttles."

"True. Especially with Ernie planning to serve Grinch cocktails at Pop's Parlor." Betty chuckled. "I don't know how I feel about drinking something green."

"Don't forget the red sugar crystals around the rim of each glass," Mist said. "And the red maraschino cherries."

"Oh, right," Betty said. "You did give him tips on how to spruce them up."

Mist and Betty waved as the van for Maisie's Daisies pulled up. The floral shop had been busy for a week, working on garlands and wreaths to decorate the tent and surrounding area. Maisie waved back quickly as she stepped out of the van. Not wasting any time, she moved to the back of the vehicle and opened the double doors. Clayton, her husband and the town's fire captain, came around the other side and began carrying greenery over to the tent area.

"Do you think they need help?" Betty said.

Mist shook her head lightly, just enough to make her earrings—long copper hoops with swirled Czech glass teardrops—sway. "I asked her when I picked up the order for the hotel. She said Clayton's help would be enough."

"It's good his parents are in town to watch Clay Jr., that little rascal." Betty chuckled again.

"A very good point." Mist laughed along with Betty. Maisie and Clayton's two-and-a-half-year-old son had proven to be precocious, extremely curious, and eager to get into anything he could get his hands on.

The two women began to walk in the direction of the hotel, a short stroll that soon led them quickly to the elegant yet cozy lodging establishment. The exterior of the building looked even more festive than it had in past years. Clive, Betty's beau and owner of the local gem and art gallery, had outlined the second-story windows with lights, as well as running a string along the roofline. With twinkling garlands on the front porch railings, the wreath of silver bells on the front door, and a stately Christmas tree inside the large front window, the overall effect was that of a fairy tale.

Inside, Mist and Betty took seats at the center island of the kitchen, which served as a prep table for cooking at times and a place for staff and close friends to gather for coffee, tea, or simply conversation. In addition, most of the planning for guest arrivals and meals took place at the island's countertop.

"I'm glad you'll have help with the Christmas Eve dinner this year," Betty said. "It will be challenging having two seatings." Her eyes settled on a second reservation binder sitting alongside the usual registration book for hotel bookings.

"Challenges in life are simply adventures in disguise," Mist responded. "Besides," she added on a more pragmatic note, "the two young women coming to help are hoping to start their own catering company. It will be good practice for them. And having two seatings is the only way to accommodate the demand this year with so many coming into town for the festival."

"That's because the reputation of the Moonglow Café has spread over the years," Betty pointed out. "And the shuttles coming into town for the festival are making it easier for visitors to add the Christmas Eve meal to their visit. It was a smart move to require reservations this year. You saw how quickly they filled up."

Mist remained quiet as she opened the café's reservation binder and looked over the dinner seating lists.

Betty reached out and patted Mist's hand. "I know you're discouraged about turning people away."

"It wasn't easy," Mist admitted. "But there are only so many tables, and I still feel not expanding into the front parlor was the right decision. Overnight guests deserve to have that space open to relax and visit, just like other years."

"And dinner guests for each seating may linger after the meal," Betty said. "So that room will give them a place to congregate."

"Yes. We'll serve dessert in the front parlor to help keep the main dining room on schedule." A slight crease formed on her forehead, just enough for Betty to notice.

"You don't care for that word 'schedule' do you?"

Mist looked up and smiled. "You know me well by now."

"You like life to... how do you put it? To flow."

"Yes," Mist said. "According to its own rhythm. But I also understand a larger crowd can bring a different rhythm."

"I believe the word for that is chaos," a deep voice boomed as Clive entered the kitchen through the back door. He stomped his boots on the doormat to shake off a light layer of snow before stepping completely inside.

"Chaos and serenity can find a balance."

"If you believe it, Mist, I believe it," Clive said. He shrugged his jacket off, hung it on a hook behind the door, and followed the aroma of freshly brewed coffee to the kitchen counter. By the time he reached the pot, Betty had already poured him a cup. "Thank you, my dear," he said, giving her an affectionate peck on the cheek. He took a seat at the center island. "So, what are we worrying about at the moment? I can tell by the expressions on both your faces that something's amiss."

"Not really, Clive," Betty said. "We were just discussing how hard it is to turn people away for Christmas Eve dinner. Even with two seatings this year, we can't take everyone."

"They'll survive," Clive said. "The caterers in the big tent are planning quite a spread, I understand. And William Guthrie is planning to serve something at a side booth."

Betty and Mist exchanged looks, which Clive picked up on immediately. No one within miles of Timberton trusted food from the old greasy spoon Wild Bill's.

"Now don't you worry," Clive said. "Bill is making his famous chili. It's the one thing on his menu that he usually gets right. And it'll warm people up on a cold December evening."

"That's actually a good plan," Mist said. "Not everyone wants a fancy meal. I like the idea of something for everyone. We'll provide the elegant meal here at the hotel, William Guthrie can contribute his chili, and the caterers for the tent area will offer fare that ranges between the two.

"You'll save a plate for me, won't you, Mist?" Clive pursed his lips as if pouting at the idea of missing the hotel's legendary meal. "I'll need to keep the gallery open so folks can wander in and out."

"Rest assured, Clive, you won't miss out," Betty said as she patted Clive's hand. "If you behave between now and then, we just might deliver it to you and even allow you dessert."

Clive raised one hand in the air as if taking an oath. "I promise to be on my best behavior."

"In any case, the second seating isn't until seven," Betty said. "You won't still have the gallery open, will you?"

Clive shook his head. "No, it'll be closed by then." He lowered his arm. "Now tell me who we get to see this year."

Mist set the dinner reservation binder down and picked up the one for hotel bookings. "All the regulars—the professor, Michael, and Clara and Andrew—and quite a few first-timers."

"One mother with a young daughter," Betty said. "I think they're from Oregon somewhere. Is that right, Mist?"

"Yes, somewhere around Ashland, I believe." Mist ran one finger down a list of names. "Veronica Sanders and her five-year-old daughter, Serena. Veronica's husband passed away last year. This is their first time going away together, just the two of them."

"Mother-daughter time is very special. And it will be nice having a child here for Christmas." Betty clapped her hands. "Children are so full of wonder this time of year."

Mist looked up and smiled at the youthful enthusiasm of the hotelkeeper. "We are all full of wonder this time of year." She tucked a loose strand of hair behind one ear. "Even if we don't realize it."

"Does this include wondering what you're serving for dinner tonight? If so, I'm indeed full of wonder at the moment." Clive chuckled as he received looks from both Mist and Betty. "Well, I thought it was funny. And I *am* seriously wondering." He patted his stomach for emphasis.

"Soup," Mist said casually, knowing this was less of a description than Clive hoped for.

"Any particular kind of soup?"

Mist looked up with a mischievous twinkle in her eye. "Yes." She looked back at the reservation book and returned to the original topic. "A retired couple from New Mexico, taking an anniversary trip, and a single woman from Ocracoke Island, along the Atlantic coast."

"Something else to wonder about, Clive." Betty reached out and patted Clive's hand.

Clive harrumphed. "I'll stick to wondering about food. And about how the gallery is doing. We've been busy this year. I'd better get back." He said his goodbyes and left.

Mist closed the reservation book and set it aside. "I hear the ingredients for jalapeño cornbread calling."

TWO

"Is that fresh chopped garlic I smell?" Maisie, arms laden with flowers and branches, stepped into the kitchen.

Mist looked up from the cutting board and smiled. "Indeed it is."

"You could use a mini food processor to do that, you know."

Mist smiled. "I could. But I like the feel of ingredients in my hands, the process of preparing them, the anticipation of what they will become." She set the knife she was holding down, rinsed her hands off in the sink, and joined Maisie at the back counter where a lush spread of white orchids, red peonies, and seeded eucalyptus lay waiting.

"What do you think?" Maisie said. "I had to hide these in the flower shop's back refrigerator to make sure they didn't get mixed in with the ones for the festival."

"They're perfect, as always, Maisie. You manage to bring in the most wonderful assortments. I love the white Dendrobium orchids. They remind me of birds taking flight." Mist raised one arm and let her hand flow through the air, mimicking the image.

Maisie tilted her head to the side and looked at the orchids closely. "You're right. I can see that now. The delicate petals look like wings."

"Exactly," Mist said, lowering her arm. "Wings that might take us anywhere."

"In which case they need to take me back out to the festival setup," Maisie said, heading for the door. "I left some poinsettias on the front porch for Betty too. Have fun arranging your centerpieces."

"I certainly will," Mist said to the empty room after Maisie departed. She placed the flowers in a large bucket of water and returned to the center island, where she set the prepared garlic aside and cleaned the cutting board. In turn, she chopped celery, tomatoes, shallots, then pulled a variety of spices from a stash she kept in a cascade of wire baskets. She often touched the baskets when passing through the kitchen, allowing them to swing freely. Clive had laughed the first time she'd explained that this allowed the spice of life to flow through the hotel.

"No lack of ingredients, I see!" Betty exclaimed as she entered the kitchen. She looked in a bright red ceramic bowl filled with vegetables still to be prepped. "What kind of soup are you making anyway?"

"Everything Soup," Mist said simply.

Betty peered into a pot nearby. "With mashed potatoes on the side?"

"That will be gnocchi," Mist said. "Not on the side. But in the soup."

"I see." Betty picked up a zucchini from the bowl and waved it in the air. "Is there anything that is *not* going in the soup?"

Mist let a hint of a giggle escape. "The kitchen sink?"

"So it's everything but... Okay, I get it." Betty laughed as she put the squash back. Glancing next at the bucket of flowers, her eyes grew wide. "I see Maisie has been by. Those are gorgeous! How are you arranging them this year?"

"I'm keeping things simple. They'll surround narrow rectangular glass dishes holding rows of votive candles. I have twigs from the garden to intersperse with the flowers and greenery."

"It sounds lovely. Elegant and rustic at the same time." Betty nodded in approval. "How many townsfolk do you expect for dinner tonight? Not counting Clive and William Guthrie, never known to miss a meal."

"A dozen? Two dozen? Three dozen?" Mist's shoulders lifted and lowered in a semishrug that looked more like a soft inhale and exhale. "However many we feed tonight, there will be extra for Sally to take to the food bank." She pointed a carrot at two large pots on the stove.

An incoming phone call sent Betty hurrying out front to the registration desk. Just as quickly, she returned. "Early arrival, the woman from Ocracoke Island. She offered to stay in Bozeman to not inconvenience us, but I told her to come on in. She'll be here in about two hours. That's fine, I hope."

"Not only is it fine, but it's lovely. She can join us for dinner if she likes, and her room is ready," Mist said. "I just have to add a finishing touch."

"I'm going out to arrange the poinsettias on the front steps while you continue your magic." Betty lifted a red jacket, fitting for the season, off a hook by the back door. Donning snowflake-patterned mittens and a thick wool scarf, she left the kitchen.

Mist pulled out a large frying pan and sautéed garlic, onion, and fresh herbs. She then added that to the large pots along with the fresh chopped tomatoes and vegetable stock she'd made the day before. Bringing it to a boil, she turned the heat down to simmer and headed for the closet in the back hallway where she kept a secret stash of items to add personal touches to guest rooms.

"Battenberg lace, vintage fire truck toys, miniature copper kettles, a green mohair shawl," Mist said to the stuffed llama who guarded the treasures. "So many choices." She rummaged through several baskets and chose a book on the history of silk. Contemplating additional items for other rooms, she closed the closet and carried the book upstairs to the small room at the end of the hall where the guest from Ocracoke Island would be staying. She placed it on the antique oak dresser, turning it a slight degree to one side. "There you go, Valerie Moore," she said to the guest who had yet to arrive.

Returning to the kitchen, she checked the pots on the stove and breathed in the mixed aroma of spices. Approving, she added an array of vegetables, left the soup to simmer, and turned her attention to the orchids, peonies, and eucalyptus. Over the next hour, she created borders of petals, twigs, and greenery around the narrow glass trays she'd found at Second Hand Sally's. When she finished, she set a centerpiece on each table in the dining room and stood back. "Yes," she said. "You all look enchanting. Now we are here."

"Where exactly would that be?"

The familiar voice caused her to turn and smile. Michael Blanton, a guest for many years and now the closest thing to a soul mate that Mist could imagine, leaned casually in the doorway, hands stuffed in his pockets.

"Why, we are where we are, of course," Mist said as she crossed the room to accept an embrace and warm kiss.

"How did I know you would say something like that?" Michael laughed as he softly bestowed a second kiss on Mist's neck.

"Perhaps you've started to see the world as I do."

"Admittedly, you may have a point," Michael said. "I do look at things differently when I look through your eyes. Still, where is it we are?"

"We are ready to welcome this year's guests; that's where we are."

THREE

As much as Mist believed in not having preconceived notions about guests, Valerie Moore was not at all what she expected. The deep, husky voice that had made the reservation belonged to a mere smidgen of a woman. Barely five feet tall and of sleight frame and delicate features, she looked like a gust of wind could blow her right off the front porch if it happened to pass through. Contemplating this unlikely visual, Mist welcomed her inside and closed the hotel door quickly.

"A beautiful hotel," the woman said, confirming once and for all that the richly toned voice Mist had heard on the phone and petite body did indeed go together. She pulled a multicolored wool hat off her head and ran a hand through short gray hair. A streak of purple highlighted one side.

"Thank you," Mist said. "We're delighted to have you here. I'm Mist."

"Misty?"

"Just Mist, like a sea breeze. And this is Michael over here in the doorway." She paused while the two exchanged greetings. "How was your trip from Ocracoke Island, Ms. Moore?" She took the woman's jacket and hung it on a coatrack in the corner of the lobby.

"Please call me Valerie. And it was a long journey, but I knew it would be. We can only reach the mainland by ferry, and then there's the drive to the airport, plus my flight had two layovers."

Mist nodded, understanding. She hadn't traveled much herself but had heard many tales from weary guests upon arrival. "And then the drive here in the rental car. You must be ready to relax. May I offer you something to drink? We have coffee and tea here in the lobby, or I could bring out a glass of wine."

"Herbal tea would be wonderful as soon as I settle in," Valerie said. "And... oh my, what's that mouthwatering smell wafting through the hotel?"

"Dinner," Mist said. "We serve dinner each night in our Moonglow Café." She gestured toward the dining room just off the lobby. "Guests and townsfolk are always welcome."

"I just may have to join you. Whatever it is, it smells heavenly."

"It's Everything Soup," Mist said.

"My favorite kind." Valerie smiled. "My mother made something like that when I was growing up. She called it Leftover Soup. It was always different, always good, but I must say it never smelled like this. You must use the perfect blend of spices."

"Several, always fresh. They change from time to time," Mist said. "Like life."

"Like life." Valerie smiled. "I like that."

"Let me help with your bag," Michael said. "I'll be glad to take it to your room for you."

Valerie waved her hand in dismissal. "Thank you, but it's very light. I'll be fine."

"In that case, I'm off to see how Clive is doing at the gallery." He excused himself and slipped out the front door.

Valerie filled out a registration card, and Mist handed her a room key. Promising to return for tea, the woman went upstairs. Mist checked the selections of tea on the beverage counter, and finding everything satisfactory, returned to the kitchen, where she found Betty pouring herself a cup of coffee.

"I see our first guest has arrived," Betty noted.

"Yes. Valerie Moore. Quite intriguing, not what I expected somehow. Very artsy, which I did anticipate."

"Really," Betty said. The comment came out more as a statement than a question.

Mist made herself a cup of peppermint tea and joined Betty, both women taking seats at the center counter. "She mentioned on her phone call that she runs an artist co-op on Ocracoke Island. I looked it up and saw the beautiful silk scarves she paints and sells there."

"Hand-painted scarves?"

"Amazing designs—loggerhead turtles, dragonflies, scallop shells, and more," Mist said. "I've never painted on silk before. I must try it sometime."

"If you ever catch up with the demand for your mini-paintings," Betty pointed out. "Clive can barely keep them in stock at the gallery. Plus your custom orders."

Mist cupped her hands around the tea and breathed in the minty aroma. She exhaled, took a sip of tea, and set the mug down. "There will be time. There's always time."

Betty chuckled. "Try telling that to Marge and Millie. They're running in circles, trying to get the various booths set up for the festival. And Marge has the candy store to run too. At least the library is closed so Millie doesn't have to juggle her librarian duties."

"It will all come together," Mist said. "They'll see tomorrow night when the festival lights meet the stars."

"Yes," Betty said. "Rather poetic having the lights come on at sundown, I think."

"Brilliant in many ways!" Mist stood up, pleased with the mental image of sparkling lights and stars at twilight. "Clayton has wired them to all come on simultaneously, the tree as well as the surrounding lights. Like a burst of magic." She moved to a pantry cabinet. She pulled three covered trays of cornbread out, along with a large basket draped with gingham cloth. "We'll warm these up right before people arrive. The basket will hold plenty, and we can refill it if needed."

Betty pulled the reservation book over and flipped it open to a bookmarked page. "The rest of the guests all arrive tomorrow. We have the annual cookie exchange in the afternoon. And the festival starts tomorrow evening." Betty looked up with wide eyes, as if just realizing how busy it would be. "It's going to be hectic!"

"Maybe hectic is just another word for exciting," Mist suggested. "Full of the energy of life, mixed with the joy of unexpected twists."

"Leave it to you to describe what will be the busiest day of our year that way," Betty said. "But you're right. That's the attitude I'll take. Besides, everything seems very organized, thanks to all the townsfolk who volunteered to help."

"That's community," Mist said. "And Timberton will be overflowing with community spirit the next few days."

"I can hardly wait." Betty stood, finished the last of her coffee, and took the cup to the sink.

"It will be joyful," Mist said. "I'm ready."

FOUR

orning arrived shrouded in light snowfall, the sun peeking through just often enough to tease the day awake. Mist ventured out of her room early in a flowing white cotton nightdress to set coffee brewing and slide lemon poppyseed scones in the oven. As the aroma of baking floated through the air, she chose items from the hallway closet stash to place in the rooms of guests who would be arriving that day: an old compass, a set of colored pencils, a stuffed hedgehog, a jigsaw puzzle of soaring doves, and whatever else spoke to her as something that would add a personal touch.

One by one, guests arrived at the hotel, each greeted cheerfully by either Mist or Betty or, at times, both.

"What an enchanting hat you're wearing," Mist said to five-year-old Serena Talbot as she stepped through the front door with her mother. "I love the pig design with all the surrounding leaves. He must be exploring a forest."

"That's Biscuit," the young girl said. She patted her head, one hand landing accurately on the pig in what Mist guessed was a well-practiced move.

"Oh, it is?" Mist leaned forward and introduced herself to Biscuit, addressing the soft wool directly.

"She named him after her favorite pig at our potbellied pig rescue," the woman behind the child said. "I'm Veronica. We're delighted to be here." Tall and lithe, with soft brown eyes and flowing hair to match, she appeared to Mist as a dancer in winter street clothes might, or perhaps even an ethereal being from another dimension. Her daughter evoked a similar feeling.

"And we are delighted to have all three of you as our guests," Mist said. Serena looked up at her mother and smiled. "Let me show you to your room." She lowered her voice to a whisper. "It's my favorite," she whispered to Serena.

"Your favorite?" Serena whispered back.

"Oh, definitely," Mist assured her. It was the truth. After all, every room was her favorite.

Mist had barely returned downstairs before the front door opened again, and Clara Winslow walked in, along with her recently found second love, Andrew.

"It is so good to see you again!" Clara exclaimed as she and Mist exchanged a warm embrace. Her mittened hands patted Mist's back as a mother might pat a child. Andrew set their bags down on the floor and shook hands with Clive, who had just entered from the kitchen.

"Hovering in the kitchen as always, I see," Andrew joked. Clive's penchant for food-searching was hardly a secret.

"Of course!" Clive answered. "You never know what sort of scone or brownie might fall off the counter into my hands. I have to be ready."

"A good philosophy," Mist said, stepping back as she and Clara released their embrace. Her work boots made a light shuffling sound beneath the calf-length paisley rayon skirt she wore.

"Hovering for food?" Andrew asked, one eyebrow raised. "It sounds like a reasonable philosophy to me."

Mist smiled. "Being ready for the unexpected."

"Well, we can always count on that, right?" Clara removed her mittens and let Clive take her coat. "Every year is a little bit different."

"As it should be," Mist said.

"Tell us about this Yuletide festival that's happening this year," Clara said. "I can hardly believe we get to have all the usual delights of staying here plus a festival on top of that! We saw a flurry of activity as we drove in."

"It's a lot of work." Clive grumbled but not without a look of pride.

"Joyful work," Mist clarified as she sent Clive a teasing look.

"Joy, joy, joy!" Clive chirped while rubbing his hands together.

"Oh, hush, Clive," Clara said. "We know you love all this commotion."

Clive rolled his eyes and then shrugged his shoulders. "Of course."

"The festival will be a celebration of all that is Christmas," Mist said. "This evening will include a tree lighting, carolers, and a chance to wander around with hot mulled wine or hot chocolate and take in the holiday atmosphere. Tomorrow starts with a parade and continues throughout the day with a visit from Santa, musical presentations, a Living Nativity scene with local children, raffles and prizes, and all sorts of delicious food and beverage offerings."

"But you'll be here, preparing the Christmas Eve meal," Clara pointed out.

Mist nodded, and two rose quartz crystals swung from her earlobes. "Yes, but there's an excellent catering company from Helena handling everything in the food tent."

"And Wild Bill will have his chili out there too," Clive said.

"Don't scare me, Clive." Clara laughed.

"Not trying to scare you, just giving you options. He actually does a good job with his chili," Clive said. "And *only* with his chili." He chuckled.

"I believe I'll stick with Mist's famous Christmas Eve dinner. Can you say what we're having, or is it a surprise?"

Mist laughed. "No surprise, though I always hope taste buds will be surprised by flavors, and eyes surprised by aesthetic presentation. But we're having two seatings this year, more dinner guests than we've had in the past. I printed the menu in advance to make sure guests could tell us if they had special dietary needs." She lifted a small paper from a stack on the registration counter and handed it to Clara.

Christmas Eve at the Moonglow Café

Winter Citrus Salad with Toasted Almonds
Butter Lettuce with Dijon Vinaigrette
Marmalade-Glazed Ham
Spinach-and-Mushroom Strudel
Maple Chestnut Roast with Candied Carrots
Brussels Sprouts au Gratin
Garlic-Rosemary Rolls
Caramelized Shallots with Thyme
Gingerbread Cheesecake with Pecan-Graham Crust

"Oh my," Clara said. "This looks delicious! I can hardly wait. I'm going to have to just nibble between now and then so I'll have room to try everything."

"Shall I hide the chocolate-cranberry mini-cakes I'm planning to set out in the front parlor tonight?" Mist said in a teasing voice.

Clara feigned shock that quickly turned to laughter. "Of course not. No need to go to extremes!"

"Clive and I will be glad to eat those mini-cakes for you," Andrew said.

"Absolutely," Clive said. "Anything for a good cause."

"That's very generous of both of you," Clara said. "But I believe it won't be necessary."

"Are those rascals, Michael and Nigel, here yet?" Andrew asked. "Nigel sent me an email challenging me to a chess game. Michael is to play the winner."

"Michael is around somewhere," Mist said. "The professor is coming in this afternoon."

"Lovely," Clara said. "I can hardly wait to see everyone. There's always so much to catch up on, seeing each other only once a year."

"You'll enjoy our new guests this year too, Clara," Mist said. "Some are already here. Two are yet to arrive."

Clara tapped Andrew on the shoulder. "Why don't we get settled in, dear?"

"Your usual room," Mist said, handing them the key. "Let me know if you need anything. I'll be in the café helping Betty set up for her annual cookie exchange."

FIVE

Mist stood in the kitchen door, one slender hand lightly touching the doorframe, and watched the activity in the café. It warmed her heart to see Betty entertain other locals, to hear the cheerful chatter, to listen to shared stories about family recipes as each participant contributed a batch of something delicious. The annual cookie exchange was Betty's pride and joy, a yearly activity she'd held long before Mist came to Timberton.

"I can only stay a few minutes," Marge said as she swooped in with a cellophane-covered plate. Her hair was clipped up away from her face, and she wore a work apron with a candy cane print. "The shop is busy today. Thank heavens I have two extra workers to help with candy sales during the holidays. I just had to get these buttercream candies over here to share."

Betty took the cookies with one hand and gave Marge a one-armed hug. A blinking nose from a reindeer on Betty's sweatshirt flashed a red light against the cellophane covering the plate. "So happy you could make it. These look delicious!"

"They're not all for you," Marge said, teasingly. She pulled a wrapped caramel from an apron pocket and handed it to Betty. "This will have to do for now." Both women laughed.

Marge was soon joined by Millie, who held a tray of chocolate crinkle cookies. Clayton's mother followed with a tray of coconut almond treats. The enthusiastic arrival of participants continued, and selections on the tables grew. Gingerbread men and women, chocolate fudge, and baked confections of all sorts soon filled the room, and assortments came together for each person to take home. Much of the conversation centered around the upcoming activity of the evening. All the regular townsfolk had a part to play for the Yuletide festival.

"My red cape with faux fur is ready for tonight," Sally said as she added sugar cookies to a decorated container she held. "I was so pleased to see that come into our thrift shop last month. It's just perfect for caroling."

Mist smiled, overhearing the comment. She'd had her eye on the same cape at Second Hand Sally's but knew from the way Sally had held it lovingly while showing it to her that it was meant to be hers. The sight of the container being filled pleased her as well. The mistletoe design she'd painted on the lightweight cardboard gift boxes had been just the right touch.

"I love this event," Betty said, taking a break to stop by the kitchen door and visit with Mist.

"And they love it just as much," Mist said. "That's one of the lovely things about tradition. We get to look forward to the event, and we get to look back fondly on the memories."

Betty nodded as she waved to Marge, who was hurrying back to her shop. "I'm certainly looking forward to it," she said. "Even if only to see Clive dressed in that Santa Claus outfit you made him."

"I believe a camera is in order," Mist said.

"You'd better believe it." Betty laughed. "I'm not missing the chance to capture that."

Mist glanced across the café, noting that the last overnight guests had arrived. Excusing herself, she headed to the registration desk to check them in.

"Welcome to the Timberton Hotel," Mist said as she stepped into the lobby. The couple, a kindly-looking pair in their late sixties or early seventies, wore heavy down coats and mittens too cumbersome for the relatively mild winter weather outside. She fought back a giggle as she was reminded of Ralphie's brother in *A Christmas Story*, bundled up more than necessary.

"Looks like we carried the winter gear concept a bit too far," the woman said, a sweet smile peeking out from below a brim of wool that partially covered her eyes. "We've never vacationed in the snow before."

"Winters here can be cold, but our weather is fairly mild right now," Mist said, knowing from their comment that the pair checking in were Tim and Rebecca Collins from New Mexico.

"That's a good thing for your town's festival, I imagine," Rebecca said. She removed her knit cap, and a cascade of soft brown curls fell to frame striking blue eyes.

"Yes. It will be colder after the sun goes down but still comfortable enough to be enjoyable." She handed them a registration card, which Tim quickly filled out and gave back.

"Quite a commotion you have going on in there," Rebecca said, glancing toward the café. "How fun to see everyone in the holiday spirit."

"Our hotelkeeper, Betty, has a cookie exchange every year," Mist said before lowering her voice somewhat mysteriously. "Don't worry, some of the cookies always seem to end up out here later on." She extended an arm in the direction of the refreshment area of the lobby, which was always kept stocked with beverages and treats for guests. As she lowered her arm, the front door opened.

"Brilliant to be home!"

Mist looked over at the new arrival and smiled. "Professor, delighted to have you here. Come meet Tim and Rebecca, two of our new guests this year." She turned to the couple. "This is Nigel Hennessy, who charms us with his presence each year."

"And his accent, I imagine," Rebecca said. "Are you from England perhaps?"

"Indeed I am," the professor said. "But I live in Missoula now, not far from here. I teach at the university there." He shook hands with both guests. "You've come to stay at the most wonderful place, I assure you."

"We're thrilled to be here," Tim said. Rebecca nodded in agreement.

"Pleased to meet you both." The professor turned toward Mist and pointed up the stairs.

Mist laughed. "Yes, your usual room. I'll bring your favorite tea and biscuits up in a bit."

"Brilliant!" With a quick "See you all later," the professor disappeared up the stairs.

"Why, it feels like family here!" Rebecca exclaimed. "I already feel at home."

"We *are* family," Mist said, "and that now includes both of you. Let me show you to your room, a lovely suite on the second floor. You can settle in and then relax in the front parlor or wander through the town. We'll serve a simple dinner in the café tonight, or you'll be able to pick up something delicious at the festival's food tent."

"Will there be carolers, do you know?" Rebecca asked. "I do love Christmas carols. I hope they sing 'The Little Drummer Boy.'" She hummed a soft pa rum pum pum pum.

"You can count on it," Mist said.

"It looks like we can count on a wonderful Christmas," Tim said.

Mist smiled as they all started up the stairs. It was always a wonderful Christmas at the Timberton Hotel. And this year it would be the same for Rebecca and Tim as well.

SIX

Mist surveyed Betty's outfit from head to toe and smiled. Red velvet flowed lovingly over the hotelkeeper's ample figure, the dress trimmed above and below with white faux fur. The accompanying red ruffled bonnet featured a sweet white lace that matched that of the white apron that fell from her waistline. A few soft tendrils of gray hair had escaped from the cap, giving Betty an appearance more youthful than her senior years. She looked perfect, exactly the way Mist had imagined.

"I believe you're the most beautiful Mrs. Claus I've ever seen," Mist said.

Betty swooshed her hand in dismissal of the compliment yet, at the same time, beamed with pride. "Thanks to your clever sewing skills."

"The costume is just the wrapping," Mist replied. "The real beauty is inside."

"Sweet of you to say," Betty said. "I must admit I do feel elegant what with all this velvet and lace around me. And I can't wait to see Clive. He's changing at the studio."

"You'll make a handsome couple," Mist said. She stepped forward and adjusted Betty's cap. "I told Michael he must get a picture of you together. A memento the two of you can keep."

"You should have heard Clive earlier, saying he doubted he'd need to use all the padding you gave him." Betty laughed. "Blames it on your cooking."

Mist smiled. "I can't take all the blame. He's not one to miss a meal. But he *will* need the padding. The waist on that Santa Claus suit is purposely wide."

"I just wish we could use that cute little elf costume you made," Betty said, her expression wistful. "The peppermint candy buttons on the green jumper are adorable, and it was so clever of you to use red-and-white-striped fabric for the Santa hat. It's a shame the schoolgirl who planned to be the elf tonight fell ill this afternoon."

"Her mother said it's just nerves, that it happens every Christmas," Mist said. "I was like that as a child. The wonder of the season always seemed too magnificent. In any case, a solution has presented itself."

"You don't say." Betty raised her eyebrows in an expression of mixed surprise and delight.

"Yes. In fact, let me go see if our little elf is ready." Mist left the kitchen and, in a matter of minutes, returned, accompanied by a petite figure. "I present to you Serena the Elf."

"The magical elf," Serena whispered to Mist, who bent down to hear the important message from the child whose hand she held.

"Oh, yes, of course!" Mist straightened up and brought her free hand to her chest. "Serena the Magical Elf," she said. "How silly of me. I believe I was simply confused. It's not every day magical elves come to the Timberton Hotel."

Serena smiled, pleased with Mist's clarification. She looked eagerly at Betty. "Do I get to be your helper?"

Betty smoothed the front of her white apron with both hands. "I would love that, and I know Santa would too. He's very fond of magical elves." She and Mist exchanged smiles as if to confirm this new trait of Clive's they had just established.

A polite knock on the kitchen door preceded Veronica's entry. "Here's the bag that goes with your outfit." She placed a long strap of fabric candy canes over Serena's shoulder and head, letting the bag rest against the child's opposite side where it wouldn't fall off.

"You'll be going with us, I hope," Betty said to the girl's mother.

"Definitely," Veronica said. "I wouldn't miss it." Lowering her voice, she added, "And I want to be sure not too much magic happens all at once. Magical elves can get quite excited at times." She winked, and Betty and Mist both smiled.

"Have fun, magical elf!" Mist directed her comment to Serena.

"You won't be joining us?" Veronica asked as she helped her elf daughter into a jacket.

"I will later," Mist said. "A few of the townspeople are planning to come to the café for dinner, and I want to make sure they are fed. Most will be eating at the festival. The caterers have arranged a nice assortment of options."

Veronica nodded. "I'll have to check that out tonight. Then tomorrow we'll join you for the Christmas Eve meal here, which we've heard so much about."

"Shall we go find Santa?" Betty said with a Mrs. Claus voice she'd been practicing. Bundling up for the cold, Betty, Serena, and Veronica headed out.

Mist turned her attention to the café, setting out a light buffet of sandwich makings, salads, condiments, and cupcakes, keeping the meal equally as casual as the following night's would be elegant. The café's traditional "Pay what your heart tells you" container and sign near the doorway handled financial matters, and the buffet-style presentation allowed guests to serve themselves. With careful planning and most of the food prep done ahead of time, meals at the Moonglow Café were often much easier than they appeared. Cleaning up, doing dishes, and all the assorted post-meal tasks could be done in their own time, after customers departed.

Assured everything was in place, Mist stood back to inspect the café one more time.

"I'm taking over."

Maisie's voice broke the silence, and Mist realized she'd been so absorbed with the room arrangements that she hadn't heard Maisie enter through the kitchen door.

"You sound quite certain," Mist said, surprised at Maisie's firm statement.

"I am," Maisie said. "I've been out there all day setting up, and I need a change of pace. And you should really see the tree lighting. It will be magnificent. The strings of lights wind all the way to the tips of the branches. Speaking of magnificent, these centerpieces are amazing. The orchids and peonies are beautiful together."

"I get my flowers from the most wonderful florist in all of Montana," Mist said. She leaned to one side and peeked behind Maisie's back. Then, with a touch of dramatic flair, she tilted her head and checked the opposite side. "What about Clay Jr.?"

"Clay's parents are watching him."

"And Clay's parents?"

"Clay is watching *them*." Maisie laughed. "Everyone is watching everyone, and you need to be watching the… what is it you tell people? Oh, the 'lights meet the stars.'"

Mist took another survey of the buffet. Everything was ready, and Maisie knew her way around the kitchen from helping with meals many times in the past. "That would indeed be lovely," she mused.

"Yes, it would," Maisie said. "Plus there's a magical elf out there somewhere who is wondering if you'll be coming out."

"I see," Mist said, fighting back a smile. "In that case, I suppose I should make an appearance. I'll grab my cape and gloves from my room and head right over." She took one more look around the room, thanked Maisie, and left.

SEVEN

A buzz of anticipation hovered in the air, flowing from the gathering in the center of town, mixing with light snowflakes falling from the sky. Mist felt the energy immediately the moment she stepped out onto the hotel's porch. Even two blocks away, the current was palpable and enticing.

She took her time walking, enjoying the laughter that grew louder as she approached and then louder again as she joined the crowd. Excited voices exchanged tidbits of conversation, waiting for the central tree to light up, and children stood on tiptoes, watching for Santa to arrive.

Ernie, from Pop's Parlor, passed by, offering her a Grinch cocktail from a tray he was carrying through the crowd. Mist, feeling the chill of the winter night, politely declined, saying she thought she heard the hot cocoa booth calling her name. After Ernie moved on, she took a look at the long line for the warm chocolaty beverages and decided to wait until she returned to the hotel. The front lobby offered not only coffee and tea but hot chocolate and cider as well.

She felt an arm slide around her waist, and she smiled. She knew the gentle nature of Michael's touch, could recognize it without even looking up to see the source. She leaned against him, keeping her eyes on the cheerful scene.

"An excellent turnout," Michael said. "There must be at least five hundred people here."

"Quite amazing," Mist agreed. "To think all these people have come out on a cold winter evening to share the holiday spirit together, many locals but also many from afar."

"Strangers," Michael mused.

"Not anymore," Mist said. "As soon as they entered Timberton, they became friends. They may not know it yet, but they are. This town brings people together even if they're unaware it's happening."

"I believe you," Michael said. "I've seen it happen."

Mist turned to look at Michael for the first time since he'd approached. The illumination from the town's streetlamps, kept low to contrast with the upcoming tree lighting, cast a soft glow across his features, giving depth to his gray-green eyes, a shade Mist likened to patina. "Life is simply amazing," she said.

Michael cupped one hand around Mist's face, brought her lips to his, and then spoke. "I love the way you look at the world, Mist. So full of wonder."

"It is full of wonder. We just have to keep our eyes and hearts open to see it." Mist and Michael both turned toward a voice starting up on a loud speaker.

"Welcome, everyone!" Clayton, assuming co-roles as fire captain and unofficial mayor, greeted the crowd from an elevated wooden platform. A tall chair, surrounded by gifts and flanked on one side by a brightly-colored nutcracker, waited behind him for the featured guest of the evening. "We're delighted you could all be here for the opening evening of our Yuletide festival." A round of applause followed, as well a sweet shout of "Daddy!" that added laughter to the already enthusiastic response.

"Clay Jr. must be so proud to see his father up there on the stage," Michael said.

"I'm sure he is." Mist smiled, imagining the child, far too small to be seen through the crowd, jumping up and down in front of the stage.

A short beep of feedback from the microphone was quickly corrected, and Clayton continued. "We have an exciting evening ahead of us tonight."

"He sounds like a game show host," Michael whispered in Mist's ear, earning a playful elbow in his side.

"I have it on good authority that Santa will be here soon, as well as some wonderful carolers who are kind enough to brave the cold for your musical enjoyment," Clayton continued. "Are we all ready for a fun evening?" Again, applause followed his comments.

"You're right," Mist whispered, stifling a giggle as she received a reciprocal elbow nudge from Michael.

"Who's going to help me?" Clayton began a countdown from ten, clapping his hands together with each descending number as the crowd joined in. As soon as the final count was shouted, a burst of illumination filled the square as tiny white lights sprung to life on the town's giant sycamore tree and surrounding foliage, fences, and lampposts. Clayton raised a thumbs-up in the direction of the candy store.

"A thank-you to his crew, I take it." Mist looked over at Marge's shop to see two of the town's firemen waving back at Clayton.

"Exactly right," Michael said. "They were checking the wiring and switches earlier to make sure nothing went wrong."

The honk of a deep-toned horn preceded the sight of an old pickup pulling up to the curb as loud speakers played "Here Comes Santa Claus." A wreath decorated the front grate, and pine boughs graced the sides of the truck bed as they hung in scalloped fashion. Seated on hay bales, Santa, Mrs. Claus, and one adorable young elf waved to a cheering crowd before stepping down and taking their places on the stage.

"Now there's a scene that will take you back to childhood," Michael said as young children and their parents waited in line for a turn to visit with the jolly guest of honor himself.

"Serena was so excited about getting to be the elf," Mist said. "You should have seen the joy on her face when I asked if she wouldn't mind filling in." Mist noted the formerly empty sack against the young girl's side, now filled with candy canes to distribute to children as they visited Santa.

"Shall we walk a bit?" Mist slid one gloved hand around the crook of Michael's elbow and placed the other on top of that one, and the two began to stroll through the crowd. Locals greeted them with well wishes, and visitors nodded and smiled as they walked by. Beneath the towering, twinkling sycamore tree, a group of carolers stood together dressed in traditional garb, their a cappella voices entertaining those passing by with renditions of "Joy to the World" and "Angels We Have Heard on High." Falling snowflakes dotted their capes and top hats, and their faces glowed rosy from the chill in the air.

"Hot chocolate sounds good, wouldn't you say?" Michael asked as he steered Mist in the appropriate direction, then around the back of the booth. Before she could suggest making their own back at the hotel, he tapped the shoulder of a woman working the booth. Smiling conspiratorially, the woman handed two cups across the rope divider that defined the space.

"How…?" Mist didn't need to form the question.

"I paid earlier, just in case you were able to break away from the hotel." Michael raised his steaming cup in the air, offering a toast.

"And if I hadn't been able to?" Mist tapped his cup with hers, started to raise the steaming beverage to her lips, and then waited before taking a sip.

"Then I suppose I would have had to drink both myself," Michael said, smiling.

"Or offer one to someone else," Mist suggested. She looked around. "Like Hollister, for example, standing over by the carolers."

Michael followed Mist's gaze and spotted the hotel's semipermanent guest. Formerly homeless, the mysterious, gentle man now lived in a cozy downstairs room, the only one with an outside entrance. It had taken months for Mist to tempt him away from a small cave under the town's railroad trestle that he called home. But a comfortable bed, indoor heat, a backup refrigerator that Mist kept carefully stocked, and a door left cracked open, all served to persuade the man to venture in and make the hotel his home.

"He can't hear the carols at all, can he?" Michael said as they walked over to offer Hollister Mist's hot chocolate.

"No," Mist said. "He can't hear or speak, but he can see the festive costumes and sense the energy of their motions. And I'm sure he hears the music in his heart."

Not unusual for the solitary man, Hollister hesitated when Mist reached out with the drink but took it from her hand when she smiled and nodded slowly. He responded with a return smile and nod, acknowledging a silent communication they'd developed over the years.

The carolers began a rendition of "The First Noel," and Mist and Michael moved on, exchanging greetings with others as the snow continued to fall. They stopped to admire a small Christmas tree decorated with handmade ornaments by local schoolchildren.

"I should get back to the hotel to see how Maisie is faring," Mist said, turning to Michael.

"And I should see if Clayton's crew needs any help." Michael leaned close to Mist's ear and whispered, "See you later?"

Mist smiled, the sensation of cool snowflakes on her cheeks contrasting with the warm blush creeping across her face. She returned the whisper. "That would be lovely."

EIGHT

"Delicious! Never tasted anything quite like it!"

The first breakfast review came, as it often did, from William Guthrie, who, in spite of owning the infamous café Wild Bill's, seemed to always be at odds with culinary basics.

"It's quiche," Mist explained. "A breakfast quiche, in this case." She fought back a grin as she refilled glasses of fresh-squeezed orange juice for Tim and Rebecca, who watched the exchange with amusement from the other side of the table.

"I made a quiche once," Wild Bill said.

"He tried." Clayton, seated at the next table, grinned. "I was one of the victims."

"Gotta say, sure didn't taste like this." Wild Bill ignored the fire captain's teasing remark. He stabbed another forkful of quiche and inspected it.

"What did you put in yours?" Mist asked. She brushed a strand of hair off her forehead with the back of one hand. The flowing sleeve of her embroidered white blouse resembled the wave of a magic wand.

"Eggs and milk, I think."

"What else?"

Wild Bill scrunched his face up, thinking as he swallowed another bite. "I guess some salt and pepper. I don't recall exactly. What all do you have in here?"

"Mushrooms, spinach, caramelized onions, and sun-dried tomatoes."

"And salt and pepper, right?" Wild Bill looked around for others to agree. Clayton, chuckling at the next table, reached over and patted Bill on the shoulder.

"Yes," Mist said. "Himalayan pink salt and some freshly ground peppercorns. And a bit of tarragon, of course." She winked at Clive, who was having as much fun listening to the exchange as the rest of those enjoying the morning meal.

"Exactly what I was thinking," Wild Bill said, eliciting good-natured laughs around the room, his own being the loudest.

"What time do the festival activities start up today?" Clara asked. Seated with Andrew and Valerie, the trio had made plans to attend together.

"Splendid question," the professor said. "We don't want to miss anything."

Valerie and Michael, seated across from him, both nodded.

"The parade starts at ten," Betty said.

"Two hours from now," Clive noted, looking at his wristwatch. "I'd better go set up the gallery for the day. Thank goodness I have some good part-time workers so I won't have to miss the parade." He chuckled as he stood and began to pick up his plate and utensils.

"No, we certainly can't have that!" Betty placed a hand on his arm. "Go. I'll take care of those. You have a busy day ahead between the gallery and the festival. I'm glad you have extra help this year."

"Yes, I'll be able to slip out for a couple of hours this afternoon."

"Take an extra spiced-plum-and-quinoa muffin with you," Mist said, nodding toward the buffet. "Santa may want a snack later."

"That's an excellent idea," Clive said. "I have a feeling he will!" He wrapped a muffin in an oversized napkin and waved on his way out. Clayton also excused himself and followed.

"Santa loves snacks," Serena piped up, then grew pensive. "I don't know about muffins though. I always leave him milk and cookies. Chocolate chip."

Mist placed a gentle hand on the young girl's head. "I think that's his favorite," she whispered. Serena smiled and nodded, as if she'd known this all along.

"Lovely music for breakfast," Tim said, noting the upbeat Christmas instrumental. "Very cheerful to start the day." He made conductor movements with one hand while holding a coffee mug with the other.

"I like your hat," Serena said, looking up at the reindeer pattern on Tim's knit cap. "I can tell that's Rudolph because his nose is red. You always wear a hat." The multiple statements came out without breaks between them in a way children are especially prone to do.

"I like hats a lot," Tim said. "How about you? Do you like hats?"

Serena wrinkled her nose. "I like them if they have animals on them. I have one with a bear wearing a Santa hat."

"Maybe you can show it to him later," Veronica suggested. "What do you think?"

"Brilliant idea," the professor said, adding his vote to the mix. "I'd like to see it too."

"Okay!" Serena beamed.

As guests finished their morning meals and either headed out or moved to the front parlor, Mist and Betty retreated to the kitchen. Mist immediately began pulling items for dinner prep out of the refrigerator, placing them on the center island.

"I'll get the dishes," Betty said, gesturing to multiple stacks by the sink. "You have your hands full today with two dinner seatings. And I have a hunch you were up late..." Betty smiled as her voice trailed off.

"Guilty," Mist said. "But not for all the romantic reasons you're imagining." Impulsively she picked up a raw button mushroom and launched it at Betty, who ducked to avoid being hit. The tiny projectile landed squarely in the sink.

"Two points, as Clive would say." Betty laughed and shook her head, nearly as surprised as Mist was herself at the silly antics.

"I've never followed sports closely, but wouldn't that be three points from over here?" Mist whisked a rubber spatula back and forth to indicate the distance between them. She lifted her shoulders lightly and then released them in a hint of a shrug. "In any case, you are right that I was up late. I wanted to prepare the strudel and glaze for the baked ham. Also the canvases for the miniature paintings I'll give the guests."

"You already know what you're going to paint for each person?"

Mist picked up an orange and contemplated it as she twisted it from side to side. "No idea." Lowering the fruit, she began to grate zest into a small ceramic dish.

"And you're not worried."

"Not at all," Mist said. "The images will come."

"And dinner for forty at four p.m.?"

Mist smiled but remained silent, knowing Betty didn't expect an answer.

"And again at seven p.m.?"

Again, Mist remained silent.

"You amaze me," Betty said, moving from one dish to the next. "I would be panicking if I tried to coordinate everything you do for our holiday guests."

"I don't think so," Mist said. "Truly, I don't. You would find exactly what I find each year."

"Which is what, exactly?"

"That everything comes together when it's supposed to."

NINE

Mist refilled the crystal bowl in the lobby with glazed cinnamon nuts. They seemed to be disappearing even faster than other years. She suspected little Serena had something to do with this, although she'd seen Valerie grab several on more than one trip through the lobby. This reminded her to put recipe cards next to the bowl so guests could take a card home and prepare the sugary treats for their family and friends.

As if hearing Mist's thoughts, Valerie peeked into the lobby from the front parlor. Dressed in jeans and a dark red sweatshirt, the green turtles on the silk scarf draped around her neck, and while not specifically a Christmas theme, it gave the outfit a holiday look.

"I believe I've become addicted to those. Any chance of getting the recipe?"

"Every chance," Mist said. She held out the bowl so Valerie could take a few more pieces, which she did without hesitation. "I'll put copies out later. Feel free to take one. They're very easy to make. We serve them every year."

Valerie finished a glazed nut that she'd been enjoying while Mist was explaining about the recipe cards. "This will be a perfect treat to have on the counter back at my gallery. Customers will love them." She gestured toward the front parlor. "Come join us. We're having the most interesting discussion. Rebecca and Tim work at the Gila Cliff Dwellings visitor center."

"How fascinating!" Mist said. "I knew she and her husband were from New Mexico but not what kind of work they do. I'll ask the brussels sprouts to give me a short break."

A faint laugh flowed from around the corner, out of sight but within earshot. "I shall hope they will not talk back."

Valerie smiled. "Your English guest is delightful, so charming and entertaining."

"Yes, we call him the professor," Mist said. "He spends every Christmas here, has for many years. We adore him."

"I can see why," Valerie said, lowering her voice. "That accent alone is music to my ears."

"Indeed, that is one of many aspects of the holiday music here."

"The instrumental carols playing in the background are wonderful too," Valerie said.

Mist tilted her head to the side as she held out the bowl of glazed nuts. "How about taking these into the parlor so they can become part of the music." Seeing a faint look of confusion from Valerie, she added an explanation. "I like to think of music as everything in the room: the voices, the pine needles on the tree, colors, mixed aromas of coffee, tea, and hot mulled cider, even silent thoughts. It all comes together as the music of companionship."

"Of course!" Valerie's eyes lit up. "I never thought of it that way before, but I see it clearly now. Our gallery is like that—salty ocean air, the pale pastels of seascapes, the smooth texture of silk, the rough edges of shells."

"Exactly." Mist smiled, pleased to feel a connection with Valerie, a reminder that new guests always brought new energy to the hotel's ambiance.

"I'll take these delicious nuts into the other room," Valerie said. "I'll add it to the... the orchestra."

Mist nodded. "I'll be right out after a short conversation with the brussels sprouts."

"Part of the music in the kitchen? I'm beginning to understand there's music in there too."

"Oh yes," Mist said. "There is music everywhere. We just need to listen to know it's there."

With that said, Mist headed back to the kitchen, not at all surprised to find Betty had been replaced with two younger, though adult, versions. Just as kindly-looking as the hotelkeeper, they wore pleasant smiles along with matching green aprons that were dark enough to mask most potential splatters of food.

"I'm so grateful for your help. I'm Mist."

The young women introduced themselves as Joy and Faith, pointing out that those were, in fact, their actual names, not nicknames for the season. Both had clean, scrubbed faces and hair securely pinned back.

"How delightfully appropriate," Mist said. "We always welcome joy and faith here at the Timberton Hotel. Of course, we welcome much more than that, but joy and faith are always in demand, especially at this time of year." She reined in her philosophical musings long enough to pull a list from the refrigerator. Replacing the starburst-shaped magnet on the appliance's metal surface, she laid the paperwork on the center island.

"With two seatings for our Christmas Eve dinner, I felt a need to list the afternoon and evening kitchen tasks." Mist ran her index finger down a detailed timeline, giving explanations along the way.

"It's very organized," Joy said. "And with three hours between each seating, the timing is perfect." The taller of the two catering helpers, her voice had an air of competence.

"Yes, we debated a two-and-a-half-hour break between but knew three hours would make it easier for the second seating to have the same fresh preparation as the first," Mist explained. "The hams, for instance."

Hunched over the task list in order to squint through thick glasses, Faith nodded. "The second can go in the oven as the first comes out."

"And this allows the mushroom strudel to be freshly baked for your second seating," Joy pointed out. "It's an ideal plan."

"It also works well for the guests," Mist said, placing the list back on the refrigerator in order to keep the center island clear for food. "Those at the first seating can be home to spend Christmas evening with their families, if they wish. And those at the second seating can enjoy more of the afternoon festival before they come to dinner."

"I see dessert is to be served in the front parlor, not the café." Faith looked to Mist for confirmation on this.

"Yes. It will let us clear the buffet in plenty of time to set it for the next seating."

"And the tables," Joy said. "People will move into the other room for dessert instead of lingering in the café. So we can turn over the place settings."

"This is even better for your guests," Faith added. "They can enjoy dessert in front of the fireplace and that gorgeous Christmas tree. We peeked at it on the way in. I love a tree with all sorts of mixed ornaments."

Joy nodded enthusiastically. "It's one of the prettiest trees I've ever seen."

"Clive and Michael—you'll meet them later, as they're well known for spontaneous visits to the kitchen—found the tree, and the hotel has collected those ornaments for years, long before I was here. Some go back to Betty's childhood." Mist felt a warm glow in her heart, pleased that the old-fashioned tree had caught the attention of the two young women.

"You'll find many guests and townsfolk choose to relax in the front parlor after their meals. I expect quite a few to join us when the festival wraps up as well." Mist indicated the dessert listing at the bottom of the task list. "So the dessert will need to be served there. We have a separate buffet set up. Don't worry, I'll be here to help with everything."

A fourth voice entered the conversation as a whoosh of cold air blew in the back door. "As will I," Maisie said. "Helping with the Christmas Eve meal here is pure joy."

"And?" Mist prompted.

Maisie laughed. "Also a well-deserved break from chasing a toddler, entertaining in-laws, and cooking at my own house."

Mist introduced Maisie and the two new helpers to each other and gave all three a quick tour of counters, cupboards, and refrigerator shelves, all of which held portions of the elaborate meal to come. "The dessert is in another refrigerator, but I'll bring that up later. You won't need to get anything that isn't in this kitchen." She and Maisie exchanged knowing glances. Hollister would likely become unsettled by strangers entering the room that served both as kitchen backup and a place for him to sleep.

"Everything is under control," Maisie said. She turned to Mist. "How about visiting with your guests while the three of us divide tasks?"

"I believe I'll take you up on that," Mist said. "I have a front parlor conversation to check in on, and a parade to view. I promised a young elf that I would be there."

Maisie waved both hands in a shooing motion. "Go then. Enjoy. I know you'll be back here checking on everything within the hour."

"You're right, of course," Mist said. "But for now… just tell the brussels sprouts thank you."

With that, she departed, leaving three very confused faces behind.

TEN

Mist found the crowd she expected in the front parlor, with the delightful addition of Michael, who sat in his favorite chair by the fireplace, book in hand. He looked up and smiled as he noted Mist's arrival.

"There she is," the professor said as Mist entered. "Do have a seat and stay for a bit. We're having the most interesting discussion about cave dwellings and potbellied pigs."

"Yes, about Biscuit!" Serena, dressed in her elf outfit, ready to leave for the pre-parade lineup, sat beside her mother. "Biscuit wouldn't want to live in a cave."

"Cliff dwellings are not quite the same as caves," Michael said.

"How do you know that?" Serena said.

"I've been to the Gila Cliff Dwellings, where Rebecca and Tim work," Michael said.

"That must be a fascinating place to work," the professor said.

"Volunteer is more accurate," Rebecca said. "We're both retired teachers. I taught history, and Tim taught music theory." She turned back to Michael. "When were you there? What did you think?"

"Were there pigs there?" Serena leaned forward, causing the pom-pom on her Santa hat to flop into her face. Veronica brushed it back and encouraged her daughter to listen.

Michael shook his head, smiling. "No pigs. Not that I saw."

Rebecca backed him up. "Michael is right. There are no pigs living in the Gila Cliff Dwellings."

Tim laughed. "I believe that question is a first, and we've been asked plenty of interesting questions at the visitor center."

"Well, that's okay," Serena said, seemingly resigned to the idea that pigs didn't live in caves, at least not in the location being discussed.

"It was fascinating," Michael said in response to Rebecca's question. "I hiked in with two cameras and a tripod, quite a hike carrying that much equipment."

"The trail is a mile-long loop," Tim explained for others.

"It was worth it, both for the photos and for the sense of the history. You could almost feel the spirits of those who lived there long ago." Michael glanced at Mist and smiled, knowing her metaphysical leanings.

Rebecca turned to Serena. "That was a really long time ago, hundreds of years."

"How many hundreds?" Serena asked.

"About seven hundred," Rebecca said.

"But no pigs lived there, right?"

Rebecca smiled. "Well, I wasn't around back then, so I can't be absolutely sure, but I don't think so."

"You really love pigs, don't you?" Valerie said.

"She has a favorite pig on the hat she was wearing when she arrived," Mist offered.

"Biscuit!" Serena beamed.

Veronica spoke up. "We run a potbellied pig rescue." She pulled a phone out of a pocket and handed it to Serena. "You can show them some photos, if you'd like."

The young girl took the phone and proceeded to work the room, introducing guests to life at the rescue. Mist, in particular, was delighted to see photos.

"Serena is very involved with our residents," Veronica continued. "She reads them stories."

"Brilliant!" the professor exclaimed. "That's great reading practice for you." He appeared to contemplate Serena's blank expression and added, "And I'm sure the pigs enjoy the stories."

"They do gather around her when she brings a book out to the cabins," Veronica said.

"Cabins?" Valerie leaned forward. "Do your pigs live in cabins?"

Serena nodded, and Veronica spoke up to clarify. "We have cabins in the pens. My late husband built them for us. They're similar to dog houses but larger. A local artist painted them different themes."

"The castle is my favorite," Serena said. "But Biscuit lives in the one that looks like a barn."

"Do you have one with a seaside theme?" Valerie asked. Serena shook her head.

Veronica's face lit up. "That's a good idea! We do have one without a theme. I think I'll ask the artist to do that."

"Let me send you a few decorations from Ocracoke," Valerie offered. "I would love to contribute something."

"How kind of you to offer!" Veronica said. "That would be wonderful." She turned to Serena. "What do you think? Should we make that last cabin a beach house?"

"Yes!" Serena clapped her hands. "Can I make a beach outside with sand?"

"I don't see why not," Veronica said.

"Then we can sell pig sand in the gift shop!"

"That might be going a little too far," Veronica said. "Let's just keep the gift shop for gifts." She turned to the group. "The gift shop helps fund the rescue efforts—food, vet bills, and other basic needs. Serena and I run it together, along with help from volunteers."

"I get to work there," Serena said. "But an adult has to help me."

"It's always good to have a bit of help," the professor said.

"Do you sell any paintings in your gift shop?" Michael asked. He sent a quick glance in Mist's direction, and she smiled in return.

"Not many," Veronica said. "A few local artists donate from time to time." She reached over and patted Serena on the knee. "I think we'd better get you down to the gallery. We don't want to hold up the parade, do we?" She turned to Mist. "That's where we meet, right? The gem gallery?"

"Yes. Santa and Mrs. Claus should be waiting for you there."

Serena hopped up and impulsively ran over to Mist, throwing her arms around her legs. "Thank you for letting me be Santa's helper!" She hugged Mist for a few seconds and stepped back.

Mist, touched by the unexpected gesture, crouched down in front of Serena so the two were at eye level. "Thank *you* for helping *him*." She adjusted the young girl's Santa hat. "You make a wonderful elf."

"I say we all go watch the parade," Michael said as he set his book aside.

"Splendid idea!" The professor stood, and the other guests followed suit, heading off to various rooms to gather coats, hats, and gloves.

"I don't suppose you can join us," Michael said, stopping near Mist, who leaned casually against the wall, watching the group depart.

Mist smiled but shook her head. "Culinary and artistic muses call."

"I thought as much." Michael laughed. "If you do manage to slip out, I'll be helping at the gallery while Clive…" He looked past Mist to make sure Serena had left. "…while Clive runs his important errands," he finished.

"We'll see," Mist said.

After a sweet exchange of kisses, Mist watched Michael leave for the festival, just as the others had done. Looking around the empty front parlor, she was struck by the sense of shared lives and conversations. Smiling, she turned away. The parlor would soon host more of the same, and as she had told Michael, her muses beckoned.

ELEVEN

A quick trip through the kitchen confirmed that Joy and Faith had the dinner meal well under control. Both hams stood glazed and dotted with whole cloves. Shallots rested in a large ceramic bowl, waiting to be caramelized later in the day.

Thanking both young women for their help, Mist retreated to her room. As if it were any other day of the year, she gave herself permission to close the world out and listen only to the murmurs of creativity. This was her personal sanctuary, one small room with only a single bed, a small dresser, two easels with brushes and paint, and a view of the property behind the hotel.

The peaceful winter scene beyond the windowpanes seemed to speak to her of colors, shapes, and personalities, all the ingredients she needed for inspiration. She watched the billowing gray clouds overhead and listened to the sighing of light wind, both offering kindly to wait until after the parade to send snow flurries down. Still, the promise of new snowfall was in the air, and with it, faint images were forming, destined for canvases on a custom easel. Clive had built for her miniature paintings several years ago.

Mist prepared her brushes and paint, lining up both soft and rich colors before her while she thought about this year's guests. Every guest who came to stay at the hotel was special, and each holiday season was unique. This year was no exception. She delighted in watching the professor's intellect, Michael's sensibilities, and Clara and Andrew's love of life mix with the diverse tableaux this year's first-time guests offered: island living, southwestern geography and history, and rescue endeavors of the porcine variety. The contrast in lifestyles was vast, yet the guests blended together perfectly. This, of course, was part of the magic of the holiday season at the Timberton Hotel.

Pale blue, bright red, silver, soft yellow...

Brush stroke by brush stroke, the varying hues intertwined as they fell from the brush in Mist's hand, held both delicately and firmly before the diminutive canvas surfaces. Only a few inches across and equal in height, the small squares were all that was needed to capture what Mist saw in her imagination.

Time lost relevance whenever Mist escaped into art, and an hour, maybe two, passed before she stood back and looked at the canvases. Awaiting only final touches that evening, the miniature paintings held exactly what she'd envisioned for each guest. In addition, a half dozen impulsive additions had joined the collection, taking up residence across the second easel.

Mist cleaned the paintbrushes and set them aside, turning her attention to an antique wardrobe that served as the room's closet, pulling out one hanger

and hooking it on one of the old oak doors. Not one
to worry about fashion, her habitual wear consisted
of comfortable, well-loved clothing. Yet she'd become
enchanted with a dress that had arrived a few months
earlier at Second Hand Sally's, a soft green-and-ivory
floral print with flutter sleeves and a hem that hit
midcalf. Sally had insisted she add a pair of red flats
that had been donated to the shop from a shoe store
that was closing in a neighboring town.

With the dress hanging ready, Mist reached into
the top drawer of her dresser and lifted out a pair of
jade earrings in a silver filigree setting. She set them
on a vintage crocheted doily next to a curved hair stick
of similar metal tone that would secure her hair in a
french twist. Satisfied she was ready for a quick change
later on, she returned to the kitchen to check on the
progress for the Christmas Eve meals.

* * *

"The first ham is in the oven," Joy said as Mist
entered the room.

"Perfect timing," Mist said, noting that three hours
remained before the first seating. "The strudel will go
in when the ham comes out. It will bake while the ham
rests." She checked the timeline on the refrigerator
to make sure she'd indicated that, pleased but not
surprised to see that her directions were accurate.

"I'll bring the gingerbread cheesecake up from the
back refrigerator myself once our guests are halfway
through dinner," Mist said. "That way it will be nice

and chilled when they're ready for dessert in the front parlor."

Joy appeared relieved. "Great. I was worried about when you'd want that out, if you'd bring it here and we'd then move it out there, or if…" Her voice faded away as Mist lifted both hands in the air, palms up, as if holding an invisible platter. Faith, slicing cucumbers, also stopped and looked.

"What you see here in my hands," Mist said, "is everything we need to worry about."

Joy and Faith exchanged glances and then looked again at Mist's bare, upturned hands.

"There's nothing there," Faith said.

"Look closer." Mist lifted her hands a little higher, tilting them slightly.

"Nothing," Joy murmured, watching Mist's hands carefully, as if expecting a magic trick.

Slowly Mist lowered her arms to her sides. "Nothing is everything, and everything is nothing. So there is no need for worry. All will be well."

Faith raised her own hands, imitating Mist's gesture.

"Do you feel how light that is?" Mist watched as Faith raised and lowered her hands, as if weighing the nothingness.

"Yes, it's very light," Faith said.

"And do you feel lighter now?"

Faith smiled. "Actually, I do! I'm going to remember that the next time I feel stressed."

"Wonderful." Mist glanced around the kitchen, noting how organized the dinner preparations were.

Although she loved creating "food for the heart," as she liked to call all meals served at the Moonglow Café, it felt freeing to have help for the final hours before the Christmas Eve meal.

"If you don't need me for a bit, I'd like to wander down to the festival and see how our guests are enjoying themselves," Mist said. "Especially one little elf in particular."

"Go," Faith said. "Enjoy the atmosphere. The crowd was so cheerful this morning, drinking hot chocolate and coffee while waiting for the parade to start."

"You should each take a break to go down there," Mist said. "There's no reason for you to miss the whole day of festivities."

"That's a wonderful suggestion," Joy said, turning from Mist to Faith. "One of us can stay to supervise the ham and finish the salads, and then we can trade off."

"Perfect." Mist smiled, pleased. Everything did feel lighter indeed.

TWELVE

Melodic notes from two violins, a viola, and a cello beckoned as Mist approached the town commons. Where a cappella voices had enchanted festivalgoers the night before, a string quartet now played an upbeat rendition of "Jingle Bell Rock." Santa hats dotted the heads of the four musicians, providing a bright red-and-white contrast to their traditional black performance attire. Two young children decked out in puffy winter jackets and matching gloves twirled carefree in front of the small stage area set up for a variety of performances throughout the day. Two mothers stood nearby, talking and laughing as they cupped their hands around hot beverages and watched the children dance.

"Mist!"

Hearing her name, Mist searched the crowd and spotted Valerie's arm outstretched above her head, gloves clutched in her hand as she waved. The hotel guest stood not far from the music stage and held a Christmas stocking in her other hand. Mist returned the greeting and walked over to join her.

"I see you've been to our library's booth to paint a stocking," Mist said, delighted to see Valerie had been by the fundraising activity. "May I see?"

"Of course!" Valerie held up the stocking, which featured a Christmas tree with shells and sand dollars for ornaments. Tiny bows, mere squiggles of red paint, brightened the serene design of green and ivory.

"It's wonderful!" Mist exclaimed. "And to be expected, I might add. I've seen photos of the silk scarves you paint for your co-op. It doesn't surprise me at all to see you've turned a plain muslin stocking into a work of art."

"Oh, shush," Valerie said modestly. "But thank you. What's wonderful is your library raising money for a literacy program. What a great idea to have that here at the festival. There's a good crowd at that booth, purchasing stockings and painting them."

"I'm so pleased to hear that," Mist said. "Our library takes pride in its efforts to help the community. Millie, our librarian, is very dedicated."

Valerie smiled. "Anything that helps teach reading is a good cause. Combining that goal with art? A fabulous mix. I'm going to suggest this to our library, maybe for the next holiday season."

A hearty "Ho, ho, ho" caused both the women to turn toward a second stage area where a jolly version of Clive in his Santa costume was seated. Betty, in her Mrs. Claus outfit, stood beside Santa, one hand on his shoulder. Serena, on Santa's other side, was offering a candy cane to a boy of similar age.

"Betty's fellow is doing a great job as Santa," Valerie said. "It can't be easy talking to one child after another, and that's after being in the parade." She pushed the cuff of her jacket back to check a square-faced wristwatch. "He has about a half hour to go, I think. The festival schedule listed visits with Santa as being from noon to two."

"That's right," Mist said, taking note of the time. The festival activities would last until five, after which the crowd would head for their homes or the homes of others or to church services or, in some cases, to the Timberton Hotel for Christmas Eve dinner at the Moonglow Café. Just two and a half hours remained before the first dinner seating.

"I want to stop by Clive's gallery to see how it's holding up with Clive out here," Mist said. "And then I need to get back to the hotel."

"Of course. You have the busiest day of all," Valerie said. "But at least go by the snowman competition. It's right over behind the library booth. Tim and Rebecca are having a blast."

Mist laughed. "I don't want to miss that. Thanks for letting me know."

"I'm so looking forward to the dinner," Valerie said. "It was so kind of your hotel to put overnight guests down for the second seating."

A new voice joined in as Clara and Andrew approached. "Yes, it's perfect planning, Mist," Clara said. "We can enjoy the whole festival and still have time to freshen up before dinner."

"While others can eat earlier and then get home to their families," Andrew added.

"Exactly the plan," Mist said, waving a goodbye as she turned away.

The snowman competition, conveniently located on the way to the gallery, was a scene straight out of a Norman Rockwell painting. Energetic figures hustled through the snow, their colorful mittens, hats, and scarves popping red, blue, and green against the snowy white background. Tim and Rebecca laughed with abandon as they pressed snow onto snow. Their lopsided creation looked adorable with a crooked carrot nose, twig arms, and accessories the festival committee had made available for the activity.

"We get an A-plus for effort, right?" Rebecca shouted as she saw Mist strolling up. "We've never built a snowman before!"

"Never?" Mist laughed. "Well, you know what they say."

"Yep," Tim said as he scooped up a mitten full of snow. "There's always a first time. In fact… there's a first time for everything, right?" With that, he packed the snow into a haphazard snowball and launched it at Rebecca, who shrieked and then quickly retaliated.

Thrilled to see the New Mexico couple celebrating winter at its fullest, Mist excused herself. Enjoying the string quartet's presentation of "Winter Wonderland" on the way out, she headed over to the gem gallery where she found an equally busy scene.

With Michael and Clive's two part-timers all helping customers, Mist had an opportunity to wander through the gallery on her own. She was often there to drop something off or pick something up but rarely on her own with uninterrupted time to browse. Adopting a playful "first time ever here" attitude, she looked around as a newcomer might. It was a game she liked to play, and on occasion, she would take the most ordinary and familiar of places—her room, the kitchen, the café—and pretend she'd never been there before. Looking around in this way, the old became new again, and the mundane often became inspiring. It was similar to another trick of the mind she entertained at times in which she closed her eyes and imagined herself in a different room, visualizing her surroundings as if they were taking form around her.

Few customers were locals, most being visitors who'd come to Timberton specifically for the Yuletide festival. This provided Mist with a sense of anonymity, and she began to browse.

A wooden display case of handcrafted silver jewelry held pendants, earrings, and bracelets, many featuring Yogo sapphires from local mines, a gem the area was known for. Some designs were classic—a leaf, a teardrop, a bird—while others were whimsical—a windmill, a hedgehog, a frying pan. All glittered under lights, strategically placed above in order to show the jewelry off at its best. These were the unique creations of the gallery owner, who happened to be out of the store at the moment. If not for it being her first time there, she would have known this to be the man currently playing Santa Claus in the town commons.

Moving to a wall beyond the display case, jewelry gave way to paintings, some large, some small. The larger pieces were by a local artist, a kind, quiet man—so she'd heard—with a uniquely Western feel that rivaled the best painters of that style, Charles Russell and Frederic Remington. Stepping around a well-dressed couple discussing a western landscape in deep gold and brown tones, Mist continued on to a grouping of smaller canvases featuring mostly themes from nature, many with holiday inspiration— winterberries, holly leaves, wreaths, and pine trees. They were petite and lighthearted, just a hint of nature amid the bold Western art and carefully crafted jewelry.

"You're doing that thing, aren't you?" a voice whispered in her ear.

"What thing would that be?"

"That thing where you pretend you've never been somewhere before."

Mist glanced around and then looked back at the handsome man standing before her. She tilted her head and smiled. "But I never *have* been here before. It's a lovely gallery."

"In that case, let me show you around." He slipped an arm around her shoulders and began to escort her through the room. "My name is Michael, by the way. I don't usually work here. I'm just helping the owner out. He had to make a trip to the North Pole."

"Well, it is that time of year," Mist said matter-of-factly.

Michael nodded. "Indeed it is. 'I will live in the past, the present, and the future. The spirits of all three shall strive within me.'"

"Spoken quite like a literature professor," Mist mused.

"Ah, well, that's my day job." Michael squeezed Mist's shoulders lightly and continued the gallery tour, making a circle back to where they started.

"And what have we here?" Mist surveyed the miniature paintings on the wall.

"Now here we have something very special," Michael said.

"Is that so?"

"More than you could possibly know." Michael slid his hand upward from Mist's shoulder, let his fingers trail along her neck, and leaned closer. "This artist is so unique, so mysteriously wonderful, if you met her, you couldn't help but fall in love with her."

Mist opened her mouth to speak but found herself unable to as an unexpected rush of emotion filled her heart. She turned to Michael and read the sincerity in his gray-green eyes. Again she tried to speak, unsure what words would come out. To her surprise, only one did.

"Dinner!"

Michael stepped back, at once surprised and amused. "What?"

Mist glanced around the busy gallery, where the unfamiliar had now grown familiar, and then looked back at Michael. Aware of the flush in her cheeks, she nearly giggled as she prefaced a quick departure just seconds later.

"Christmas Eve dinner!"

THIRTEEN

The intoxicating aroma of cloves, garlic, and rosemary greeted Mist as she slipped into the hotel through the kitchen's side door. Joy and Faith welcomed her back, at the same time reassuring her that everything was under control.

"Your friend Maisie came by and arranged the place settings in the café," Joy said. "She also checked the serving dishes on the buffet, said you'd already put out everything needed."

Mist responded as she removed her cape and hung it on a hook behind the door. "I learned long ago that a meal is more peaceful if everything to be used is laid out in advance."

"Even the serving utensils, I noticed," Faith said.

"Especially the serving utensils." Mist laughed. "Those can be the hardest things to find at the last minute. They have hiding places that no human can detect. Some utensils even become invisible just to torment a party host."

Joy and Faith exchanged knowing glances. "I've suspected as much in the past," Joy said. "We've had that happen at catering events from time to time. Rarely, thank goodness."

"And then you aren't even home to find them," Faith pointed out.

Mist peeked in the oven to check the ham, pleased to see it coming along. She then checked the refrigerator shelves, noting each side dish's stage of preparation. Grateful for size of the commercial refrigerator the hotel had acquired as the café grew in popularity, she closed the stainless steel doors and moved on to check the café itself.

It came as no surprise that Maisie had done a wonderful job arranging the place settings. Each guest had all the proper silverware, water and wine goblets, and a linen napkin gathered into a rustic yet elegant ring of wooden twigs and faux berries. Miniature china salt and pepper shakers shaped like bells—red for salt, green for pepper, both with silver painted bows—graced multiple locations on each table, placed strategically to be within each guest's reach.

Adjusting a bit of greenery here and there, Mist was delighted with the way the orchids and peonies in the centerpieces highlighted each table, waiting like performers in the wings of a theater for each votive candle to be lit. A larger centerpiece of matching design graced the buffet. Small place cards with elegant calligraphy sat in front of large platters and bowls, announcing what each dish would be once the serving dishes were whisked to the kitchen and returned, brimming with hearty holiday fare.

Mist took a last look around the café and determined it was ready aside from the tasks of setting background music and lighting candles. She would take care of these details personally, at the last minute, before opening the doors. It was her tradition to spend a few minutes alone in the café before each Christmas Eve dinner.

The front parlor appeared equally organized and just as festive. The small dessert buffet flanked a wall toward the rear of the room, its white linen tablecloth trimmed with pine garland with red ball ornaments, gold toile bows, and twinkling lights. Guests would be able to pick up gingerbread cheesecake or simply coffee and then move closer to the fireplace where a sofa and winged-back chairs offered comfortable seating. Or they might choose to stand by the old-fashioned Christmas tree that stood before the front window.

A most delightful find in the front parlor was the presence of Clara and Andrew, who sat together on the sofa. The sight of the senior couple holding hands brought joy to Mist's heart.

"We should get the fire going for you two," Mist said, noting the fireplace's carefully prepared stack of kindling and logs ready to light. She moved toward the mantel where she knew a box of matches waited behind a tall wooden nutcracker.

"No, no, dear," Clara said. "Thank you for offering, but others will be arriving later. Save the fire for everyone. We just stopped to rest a bit after all the activity at the festival."

Mist smiled. "It's wonderful, isn't it? Such a celebration of community."

"We were glad to see you out there, enjoying the atmosphere," Andrew said.

"I enjoy Christmas wherever I am," Mist said. "Whether at a festival or in the kitchen or simply taking a quiet walk alone to look at lights on houses and shops, there's always something to behold during this season."

"Like the Living Nativity at the festival!" Clara exclaimed. She turned to Andrew. "Weren't the children in it wonderful?"

Andrew nodded. "Impressive. Some of them were quite young."

"They're from a local Sunday School," Mist said. "They've prepared for months."

"You can tell they were proud of their roles," Andrew said.

"Their costumes were just precious!" Clara said. "Those robes and head scarves! So authentic and appropriate. And the stable, sweet and simple, filled with hay bales."

"They built that," Mist said. "With the help of their parents."

"Amazing!" Clara beamed as she recalled the scene.

The sound of the front door opening and closing signaled the arrival of Veronica and an elf who, although smiling, appeared ready for a nap.

"I saw you on stage with Santa," Clara said. "You did an excellent job helping him. I'm sure Mrs. Claus appreciated your help too."

Veronica mouthed the words "Thank you."

"It was so much fun!" Serena said. She began yawning before she finished the statement. After she closed her mouth again, she added, "And I saw the Grinch too. He's so funny-looking. I told him so."

"Serena?" Veronica gave her daughter a questioning look.

"It's okay, Mom," Serena said, her eyes wide. "He whispered a secret to me."

"And what was that?" Mist asked, tickled to find out what Ernie, AKA the Grinch, had told her. Conversations with children were out of his regular line of work when tending bar at Pop's Parlor. She suspected the green costume had given him some unique inspiration.

Serena giggled. "He said when he looked in the mirror this morning, he thought the very same thing."

"Oh he did, did he?" Veronica said. "And where was I during this secret conversation?"

"Right next to me," Serena said. "Talking to the lady who lives on an island. I wonder if there are pirates there? Like in *Pirates of the Caribbean?*"

"I don't think so, Serena," Veronica said.

"What made you think of that?" Mist asked, intrigued by the girl's question.

Serena looked at Mist with an *isn't that obvious* expression. "It's an island, so there's water all around it. And pirate ships live in the water."

"I do see the logic there," Andrew said.

Clara nodded, agreeing. "You could ask her when you see her later."

"A good idea," Mist said. "I'm sure she'll be happy to tell you all about living on an island. And now," she said to all, "I have a bit of work to do. Remember there's coffee, tea, and hot chocolate in the lobby, plus glazed cinnamon nuts. Please help yourselves."

Mist left the parlor and took a back hallway route to her room. Closing the door, she sat down, closed her eyes, and cleared her mind, drawing slow breaths in and then exhaling. There had been many surprises this Christmas season, as she always expected there to be. But the heartfelt words Michael had spoken at the gallery had left her speechless, not to mention blushing and flustered. It wasn't that she didn't know how he felt. She'd known for a long time, and she was certain he knew she felt the same. But the moment was so unexpected that it seemed to gather up the years they'd known each other into one moment of wonder, like a sudden burst of light.

Setting those thoughts aside as best she could, she dressed for dinner, taking a little more time than usual to fold her hair into a casual french roll and clip it in place with the silver hair stick. She added the earrings she'd chosen earlier and then stood back to view her reflection in the mirror. It was not her habit to wear makeup, but on a whim, she reached into a dresser drawer and pulled out small glass vials of hibiscus flower, beetroot, and arrowroot powders. Tapping a speck of each onto a pottery coaster, she used a brush to blend them together, adding extra specks of each as needed. When she was happy with the hue, she tapped below her cheekbones lightly with the brush, allowing just a trace of color to settle on her skin.

"There," she said, seemingly addressing a storyteller doll on her dresser. "We're ready, aren't we?" Without waiting for the ceramic figure to answer, she left her room.

FOURTEEN

Mist stood alone in the café, as she did every Christmas Eve before opening the doors to guests. This was her personal tradition, her private time, and the staff and locals all knew to leave her be. She'd always felt a connection existed between these silent moments and the joy-filled feast soon to follow, as if the calm itself gave birth to an energy that took up residence in the hearts of those who would enter.

Circling the room, she leaned over each table and brought a match to the votive candles within the arrangements of orchids, peonies, and seeded eucalyptus. She smiled as each wick accepted the offering of fire, promising to cast candlelight on the faces of those who would sit nearby. As she moved from table to table, the room took on an increasing glow that was further amplified when Mist flipped a temporary switch near the closed café doors. This brought to life dozens of strands of sparkling white lights that Clive and Clayton had carefully positioned across both the buffet and the room itself. Now illuminated with candles and twinkling lights, the Moonglow Café stood ready to welcome the eager crowd outside.

Mist added one final element to the mix—classical background music with a Christmas theme—and stepped into the kitchen to announce the café was ready. Betty, now transformed from Mrs. Claus back to the hotelkeeper everyone adored, stood waiting with Joy and Faith. Platters and bowls, brimming with holiday fare, covered the center island, ready to be moved to the buffet. Mist felt a surge of joy, knowing so many would soon enjoy the feast.

As the parade of dishes moved from the kitchen to the appropriately labeled spaces on the buffet, Mist opened the café doors and welcomed in those attending the first seating for the Christmas Eve meal.

"How lovely everything looks," the first woman said as she entered, her eyes widening at the sight of the twinkling lights and votive candles. Elegantly dressed in red with a beaded white jacket, she held the arm of a silver-haired man in equally distinguished attire.

"Welcome to Christmas Eve dinner at the Timberton Hotel," Mist said to the couple. She extended her arm to indicate they should sit wherever they'd like.

"I was thrilled we were able to get the reservation," the woman said. "It's wonderful you decided to have two seatings."

"We're delighted you could join us," Mist said. She watched the couple head for a table near the front window, then turned to greet a family of four. "Welcome," she said, just as she did to the young couple who followed that family, and to all who entered after that. With each arrival, she gestured toward the café's interior, her earrings sparkling under the lights as she turned her head from side to side.

With all the serving dishes arranged on the buffet by the time the first few guests were seated, Joy, Faith, and Betty began making the rounds to fill water and wine goblets. Mist joined in, offering other beverages to those who preferred something besides wine. At the same time, she encouraged trips to the buffet and answered questions about the dishes being served.

"Yes, the dressing on the butter lettuce is a vinaigrette. No, there is no cream."

"The strudel is vegetarian... mushrooms, yes..."

"Tarragon..."

A few guests at the first seating were locals, but for the most part, those dining at the early hour were simply visitors who had come to enjoy the special holiday meal. Conversation flowed freely between people who had arrived together. Interaction between tables remained mostly polite greetings and kind smiles. It was festive yet peaceful, with an ambiance that was unique in a soothing way. Mist was quite certain the second seating, almost entirely hotel guests and locals, would be livelier. Yet there was something lovely about seeing the café filled with unfamiliar faces, strangers sharing the same meal together.

"I'm going to set up the dessert buffet," Mist said to Joy as she passed through the kitchen. "Can I help you at all here first?" A quick glance around told her what she already suspected, that everything was on schedule.

"We're fine," Joy said. "The ham for the second seating is in the oven, and everything else is prepped. Faith is making the rounds with refills of wine, and Betty is keeping an eye on the buffet. Oh, Maisie popped in to say she'd be here by six to help turn the café settings."

Mist paused, one hand on the door, before stepping into the back hallway. "You sound calm, Joy, even peaceful."

"Thanks to you," Joy said as she held out her hands, palms up.

* * *

Mist knocked lightly before entering the room with the second refrigerator, always mindful that Hollister could be there. Although she knew he couldn't hear, she offered the gesture as a sign of respect, a reminder that his privacy was important. She then entered, not surprised to find the room unoccupied. The festival was still winding down, still offering music to... watch.

Each of the four shelves in the refrigerator held two gingerbread cheesecakes, eight in total, four for each dinner seating. Twelve petite gingerbread men circled each baked delight, a nod to whimsy as well as a guide for the four silver cake servers that waited on the dessert buffet.

Taking a plate in each hand, Mist closed the refrigerator gently with her hip and carried the cheesecakes to the front parlor, resisting the urge to swing at least one of them above her head on the way, a sly move she'd been known to pull off when working at a café during college. Grinning at the mere thought, she safely delivered the desserts to the buffet and felt an unexpected sense of relief. Although she hadn't given in to the impulse, a fleeting vision of scraping the baked confection off the hotel's hardwood floor hadn't escaped her.

"Were those actually footsteps I heard?"

Mist turned to see Michael grinning from his favorite reading chair. The fireplace nearby now glowed with warmth, enjoyed by other guests relaxing in the room. She understood the teasing comment. Her reputation for gliding soundlessly as she moved was well established.

"It must be the shoes," Mist said as Michael approached. "My work boots are well versed in the ways of magic, while these are just in training." She extended one foot and tapped the floor gently, as if telling it to remain silent.

"You look beautiful," Michael said.

"Thank you, sir," Mist quipped, pleased that the soft green-and-ivory print dress, along with the carefully selected accessories, had properly transformed her appearance from her earlier work attire.

"I might be tempted to pull that hair stick out and let your hair cascade down." Michael lifted one hand as if to follow through.

"I wouldn't suggest it," Mist said. "Loose hair and food service are not desirable companions. However, if you might be tempted to help me bring two more plates out from the back refrigerator, that could be acceptable behavior. No twirling the cheesecake over your head though."

Michael's eyebrows lifted. "I'm not sure that would even occur to me, but I promise not to attempt it."

"Then you may help me."

With Michael just behind her, Mist returned to the back refrigerator and removed a gingerbread cheesecake, handing it to Michael. Taking the second one herself, she balanced it on the flat palm of her left hand and closed the refrigerator again with her hip, in spite of having the other hand free, just for the novelty of it.

"A smooth move," Michael noted.

"Merely keeping life playful," Mist said. "Always play, remember that. It's good for our well-being, helps balance the seriousness in the world." Gesturing toward the door, she waited for Michael to move into the hallway, then followed.

"Is there a different hip trick coming up?" Michael asked, noting that the door to the room opened inward.

"Not necessary," Mist said. She slid the toe of one shoe around the door, tapped lightly, and pulled it out of the way before the door swung shut.

"Impressive," Michael said, leading the way back to the front parlor. He set the cheesecake down on the buffet, as did Mist, who then paired all four plates with the silver cake servers, arranging the desserts to the right of cake plates and forks already waiting.

"There," Mist said, looking over the sweet display. "Ginger and molasses will be the stars tonight, providing a crowning touch of spice to the evening." Satisfied the buffet was ready for self-service, she encouraged Michael to go back to mingling by the fireplace while she checked the beverage area in the lobby.

"There you are." Betty smiled as Mist entered. "I just replenished the coffee, tea, and hot cider, and I'm refilling the glazed nuts now."

"Perfect," Mist said. "The buffet in the front parlor is ready, and there's a nice fire going. A few guests are chatting around the fireplace, but there's plenty of room for others."

As they spoke, the elegant couple who'd first arrived for dinner crossed from the café to the parlor. Their faces bore the afterglow of those delighted with a culinary feast. Others followed, some stopping for a beverage, some aiming eagerly for the cheesecake, all content to wander into the welcoming front parlor on a post-dinner stroll.

"I'd say round one was a success," Betty said. She smoothed down the front of her apron, the cheerful poinsettia design adding a perfect holiday touch to the emerald-green slacks and sweater beneath it. "It's simply delightful!"

Mist looked around, pleased to see the growing flow of people from the café to the parlor. "Yes, I couldn't agree more. And even more delightful is the fact we now get to do it all over again."

FIFTEEN

Mist found Maisie in the café, moving from table to table, gathering dishes. Only a few customers remained, finishing their wine and enjoying the last bites of their meal. Maisie sent a reassuring nod to Mist that all was on track. There was no need to nudge the lingering guests toward the front parlor. There was plenty of time before the next seating.

"Lots of folks from the clean-plate club, I see," Maisie said as she stacked a dish on top of several others. "Not that I'm surprised. It smells heavenly in here."

Mist grabbed a tray from a secluded area in one corner of the room and gathered water and wine goblets from one empty table. "Would you like to eat before we set up again?" She lowered her voice to ask the question so as not to disturb the last diners.

"No, no, but thank you," Maisie said. "I'll wait. Clayton and the rest of the family will be coming to the next seating. I'll take a break and sit with them."

The last customers stood, pushed their chairs in, and inquired about the coffee and cheesecake. Mist walked them across the lobby and pointed the way to the dessert buffet, noticing the energy in the parlor had intensified in the short time since she'd been there. Lively conversation flowed between people clustered together near the Christmas tree or fireplace, or seated around the room. Forks clicked against plates, and bursts of laughter danced in all directions, mixing with background Christmas music. Some dinner guests exchanged hugs with newfound friends as they gathered their coats and headed out.

"Am I missing the fun?"

Clive's voice took Mist by surprise, as she hadn't heard him approach. She turned toward him, finding neither Santa Claus nor the usual Clive appearance. Instead, he'd managed a casual yet nicer than everyday look by donning slacks, a tailored shirt, and a cable-knit sweater. Even his hair was nicely combed and… was she imagining it? Cologne?

"Doesn't he clean up well?" Betty laughed as she joined him. "If he thinks this will get him off the hook with helping though, he's mistaken."

"Why, Clive," Mist said, teasingly, "the fun is just about to begin."

Clive balked then laughed. "I wouldn't think of leaving all the work to you ladies. Point me in the right direction."

Mist gently turned him toward the café, and Betty gave him a light push. Once all three were inside the room, Mist closed the doors and turned up the lights.

"What is the task at hand?" Clive said, looking around the room.

"It's very simple," Mist said. "Everything out and everything in."

Clive looked to Betty, who already had a stack of four plates in her arms, for clarification. "Can you translate Mist-speak for me?"

Betty added a fifth plate to the others and walked over, placing the whole stack in Clive's arms. "Not a problem, dear." She pointed to the kitchen door. "One thing at a time. This is the 'everything out' portion."

Clive rolled his eyes, gave Betty a peck on the forehead, then took the plates to the kitchen, stopping just briefly as Maisie added another three to his stack.

One area at a time, Mist, Maisie, Betty, and Clive worked together to clear dishes, move centerpieces, clean tabletops, replace votive candles, and lay out new place settings. Long before the next dinner guests were scheduled to arrive, the café looked immaculate, ready for the next group of diners.

"I'll sweep through the front parlor to pick up any stray forks, plates, or glasses," Maisie said. "Faith has been running interference from the back to keep the dessert buffet clear, so most of the plates have been cleared. In fact, many are already washed and dried."

Mist thanked Maisie and the others and then did the same in the kitchen, where Joy had just removed the ham and set it on top of the range. Faith was busy pairing serving utensils with trays and bowls, and Clive was attempting to swipe a garlic rosemary roll that had just come out of the second oven. Joy swatted his hand away playfully, and Betty patted her on the back, approving of the reprimand that she often resorted to using. Together, the group carried out the final preparations for the second seating.

"It is a joy working here!" The exclamation came from Joy, causing Mist to smile at the concept of joy finding joy, joy bringing joy, and all the possible iterations of joy in general.

"And I have faith that we'll remember today fondly." This, of course, came from Faith.

"Well, I bet…," Betty began in jest but then glanced at the kitchen's wall clock. "I bet we have second seating guests arriving already."

Mist, agreeing with Betty, moved into the café and dimmed the overhead lights, lit the candles, and took a final look around. An element of festivity filled the air of the quiet café, invisible yet a foundation already set for the meal to come. Confident that all was ready, Mist notified the kitchen to fill the buffet. She then opened the café doors again, finding an eager crowd in the lobby, many with familiar faces.

"How gorgeous!" Clara exclaimed as she entered, Andrew by her side. "Honestly, Mist, I swear each year outdoes the last. Though I don't know how that's possible when each year is already perfection."

"Thank you," Mist said. "But it is those of you here together who make the room special."

"You're being too modest," Valerie said, entering just behind Clara and Andrew. "The centerpieces alone are exquisite. And the twinkling lights, delightful."

Mist indicated a section of tables with RESERVED cards that set the area aside for overnight guests. In turn, Valerie, Veronica and Serena, Rebecca and

Timothy, Michael, and the professor found their way to that section while townsfolk gathered with family and friends at various surrounding tables. Mist greeted each local by name—Marge, from the candy store, Millie, the librarian, Glenda, from the Curl 'n Cue salon, Sally, from the thrift shop, and many more. She welcomed the few she didn't know, introducing them to others.

As the eager crowd in the café grew, water glasses were filled, and wine flowed freely. Enthusiastic guests passed through the buffet line, filling their plates with glazed ham and all the accompaniments. Each step taken earlier was repeated in order to provide a perfect Christmas Eve meal.

"Everything is lovely," Rebecca said as Mist passed by with warm garlic rosemary rolls, which even Clive was allowed to take. "This will be a wonderful memory for us." She reached over and squeezed her husband's hand.

"Absolutely," Tim agreed. "A perfect choice for an anniversary trip."

"A celebration," Mist replied to them both. "Just as it should be."

"Indeed," Valerie said. She held up her wineglass as a symbolic toast.

Mist moved on, making a point of passing by each of the hotel's overnight guests, overhearing bits of conversation that warmed her heart.

"You sound an awful lot like the Grinch," Serena said to Ernie, who sat at the next table over, close enough to hear.

"You think so?" Ernie quirked an eyebrow. "But am I as funny-looking as he is?"

Serena, dressed in red velvet and wearing a gold glitter headband, contemplated her answer carefully. "No, you look okay."

"Serena!" Veronica whispered. Rhinestone earrings reflected the candlelight as she turned toward her daughter. Her admonishment lost some of its intended effect when she smiled.

"Well, that's a relief!" Ernie answered. He swiped the back of his hand across his forehead.

"I'm not sure I agree with the little lady." William Guthrie smirked from his seat beside Ernie. He sliced a sizable bite of glazed ham, which disappeared quickly into his mouth.

"In that case, no more Grinch cocktails for you," Ernie said. "You're getting a Shirley Temple the next time you come into Pop's Parlor." William Guthrie harrumphed while several others chuckled, including Michael and the professor.

Mist caught up with Maisie, who was helping Joy and Faith replenish the spread at the buffet. She picked up a plate and held it out.

"What's this for?" Maisie asked as she took the plate from Mist.

"It's for you to enjoy a meal with your family. It's Christmas Eve, Maisie. Go."

"Is that an actual order coming from you, Mist?"

Mist fought back a smile, knowing Maisie's comment wasn't serious. "You're a person with free will. I'm merely suggesting you go sit down."

"Suggesting?"

"Strongly suggesting."

Mist checked the buffet as Maisie served herself and determined that everything was in order. She passed through the kitchen, thanked Joy and Faith for the excellent job they were doing, and continued through the back hallway to the second refrigerator. Two at a time, she carried the gingerbread cheesecakes to the buffet table in the front parlor, and then returned to the café. Almost immediately, Michael pulled her into the chair beside him.

"I wondered why this chair was empty," Mist said. She leaned back and exhaled, aware her energy was dwindling. She tried to remember the last time she'd sat down but came up empty.

"You've been flitting to and fro all day," the professor said. "Relax for a few minutes."

"Let me bring you something to eat." Michael stood up before Mist could object.

"Indeed, a great suggestion," the professor said. "I've heard the food here is quite delicious."

"Maybe just some of the winter citrus salad and vegetables."

Michael left for the buffet and returned quickly with a plate for Mist that held more options than she'd asked for yet not enough for her to protest. At the prompting of others at the table, she took a few bites, appeared pleased, and took a few more.

"Well, what do you know?" Clive said, looking at Mist, then at Maisie, and then at Betty beside him.

"We finally managed to get all three of you to sit down and enjoy the meal. You all work so hard."

"It may seem we're always working," Mist said. "But it's heartfelt work, which makes it not work at all. This year especially, thanks to Joy and Faith," Mist said. "Speaking of which…" She leaned toward Michael and whispered, "Can you find two more chairs?" She retreated into the kitchen and soon returned with the women who had so carefully followed her plans for the meal.

"A quick announcement," Mist said, addressing the café. "Well, two, actually. We have gingerbread cheesecake waiting in the front parlor for all who'd like to partake."

"Count me in!" Clive said. "I'm not one to pass up a good cheesecake."

"Or any cake," Betty added, bringing a few chuckles from those who knew Clive well.

Mist continued turned to Joy and Faith. "I'm ever so grateful to you both for your help, and I insist you join us."

"I wouldn't argue," Maisie said, grinning. "She's on a roll with orders tonight."

As Joy and Faith sat down, Mist reached for a wineglass. "Before we finish our meals and move to dessert, I'd like to thank these lovely ladies for making our Christmas Eve dinner so fabulous. To Joy and Faith."

There was no hesitation in the café as others lifted their glasses in a heartfelt toast.

"Yes! To Joy and Faith."

SIXTEEN

Bing Crosby's smooth voice filled the air with thoughts of a white Christmas, which was not just a dream to the guests and townsfolk who congregated in the front parlor. Snowflakes swirled outside the front window, a perfect backdrop for the festive Christmas tree inside.

Regulars to the Timberton Hotel already knew that a handmade ornament from Clive to Betty waited, hidden within the trees branches, for the right moment to reveal itself. Only Mist knew what this year's ornament would be, having watched Clive sneak it into the tree while she was setting out gingerbread cheesecake for those who attended the second seating of the Christmas Eve dinner. The handcrafted treasure would be a lovely addition to those he'd designed for her the past few years.

From the arched entrance to the front parlor, Mist watched the crowd gathered inside: cheerful, merry, lighthearted—everything she strived for each holiday season. Whatever everyday life offered those who came to Timberton for the holidays, it was always Mist's hope that Christmas at the hotel would be an oasis of sorts even if only for a moment in time. It wasn't meant to be an escape from reality; it was meant to be an addition, something to carry forward, the memory of it becoming a thread of inspiration.

"I see the professor and Andrew finally got around to their chess game," Betty said as she and Clive joined Mist. The two men sat at a side table, their attention focused on a wooden board between them. The professor reached out, hesitated slightly, and then moved a chess piece from one spot to another.

"My money's on the professor," Clive said.

"You never know," Mist said. "Nothing is truly predictable in life."

Clive patted Mist affectionately on the back. "We'll see about that. I predict I'll be enjoying cheesecake within the next sixty seconds." He strolled off toward the dessert buffet.

"Then again, perhaps some things are," Mist admitted.

Betty laughed. "Predictable and lovable."

"You two are wonderful together," Mist said. "Just like Clara and Andrew." She looked across the room where Clara sat near the chess game in an animated conversation with Veronica, also seated. Both women balanced dessert plates on their laps.

"I remember how tough Christmas was after her first husband passed away," Betty said. "They celebrated many holidays here together. Yet she managed to find love again."

"Like I said, unpredictable."

"And then there's that fellow over there by the fireplace..." Betty nodded toward Michael, who held a copy of *The Grinch Who Stole Christmas*, Serena curled up at his feet while he read the story out loud. "You just have to love someone who reads books to children."

Mist smiled but said nothing.

"Makes one wonder what the future might hold," Betty hinted.

Mist's smile grew into a grin. "Like I said…"

"I know. I know. But I dare say not *completely* unpredictable." Betty chuckled. "I'm going to see how clean-up is coming along in the kitchen."

"Let me know if they need help."

"Absolutely… not." Betty laughed again as she retreated back through the lobby.

Mist shook her head, both amused and pleased at the efforts people were taking to make sure she relaxed and enjoyed the evening. She looked around the room again and spotted Valerie on the couch near the fireplace, sipping coffee while watching Michael read to Serena. She crossed the room and asked if she might like a refill.

"No, but thank you, Mist. This is such a perfect evening," Valerie said. "Relaxing, filled with happy faces, delicious food, sentimental music, snow falling outside… I usually stay home for the holidays, which is nice in its own way. But I wanted something wintery this year, and I can't imagine anywhere I'd rather be than right here."

"I'm so glad you decided to spend Christmas with us," Mist said. "I imagine it's different on Ocracoke Island."

Valerie took another sip of coffee. "Yes, but wonderful in its own way. The scenery is not at all the same, of course. We don't have the snowfall you have here. But we have community events, tree-lighting, concerts, toy drives, and plenty of holiday cheer. And you can walk on the beach or visit the Ocracoke Lighthouse. It's Christmas with an island twist."

"But do you have pirates?" Serena asked, having caught the end of Valerie's statement just as Michael finished reading to her.

"Pirates?" Valerie smiled. "No, though we did have a very famous pirate in the past. His name was Blackbeard. That was a very long time ago, over three hundred years."

Serena's face lit up. "Was he cool like Jack Sparrow in *Pirates of the Caribbean?*"

"I... don't think quite as cool," Valerie said. "Real life is not always the same as what you see in the movies."

"Did I hear mention of pirates?" Andrew dropped into a chair close by. "I wanted to be a pirate when I grew up. Either that or a fireman."

Valerie raised her hand. "Ballerina here."

"I always knew I wanted to be a teacher," Michael said.

As Bing Crosby's voice faded away, Frank Sinatra took over with "Have Yourself a Merry Little Christmas." Mist saw Clive wander over to the Christmas tree, and she excused herself to go in search of Betty. She found her in the lobby, tidying up the beverage area and escorted her to the living room, delivering her as if adding a present to those already under the tree. Betty, wise to the coming scene after so many years, coyly played at admiring the tree in general.

"You're quite taken with the tree," Clive teased. Arms folded in front of him, he looked round the room nonchalantly.

"Well, it *is* a lovely tree, Clive," Betty said. "Somehow each year's tree is more magnificent than the last. I'm not sure how that's possible, but it does seem to be true."

Mist surveyed the tree, agreeing with Betty's sentiment. "Perhaps we are the ones who become more magnificent with each passing year."

"And a little grayer?" Betty raised one hand and patted her hair.

"Just another touch of magnificence," Mist said.

Clive reached between the tree's branches to a spot far in the back, taking care not to disturb ornaments on the way. When he brought his arm back out, a silver trio of candles dangled from his fingertips, which he presented to Betty. As it did each year, the ornament featured tiny Yogo sapphires, locally mined.

"I adore it!" Betty exclaimed, taking the handcrafted ornament into her hand. "And the flames are beautiful, each with its own sparkling gem!" She let it twirl from her fingertips for several seconds and then placed it back in the tree alongside the others Clive had made over the past few years: a snowman, reindeer, wreath, tree, and silver bells.

"I wonder what he'll design for you next year?" Mist cast an impish grin at Clive.

"She'll have to stick with me for another year to find out," Clive said.

Betty tapped a finger against her cheek. "I just might do that."

Rebecca approached Mist and leaned closer, cupping her hand. "I think Tim could be convinced to play some carols if people'd like to sing along."

"That would be wonderful!" Mist replied. "We love seeing the piano enjoyed."

"Very true!" Betty said. "How delightful!"

"I'll go turn the music off." Mist moved to the small closet where the sound system controls were housed. Rebecca went off to borrow Tim from a serious discussion with Michael about Charles Dickens' *A Christmas Carol*. Soon guests and townsfolk alike were gathered around the piano, and voices filled the room.

"A lovely evening of celebration," Betty said as Mist returned to her side.

"Yes, and more tomorrow," Mist said, envisioning the Christmas-morning scene to come. "I believe I'll slip away now, if you don't mind. I have more preparations to attend to."

"Of course." Betty smiled, aware of Mist's Christmas-morning traditions.

Mist circled the room, pleased to see the hotel guests either participating in or enjoying the sounds of song and laughter. She paused behind Michael's chair just long enough to rest her hands on his shoulders. He reached up and took both her hands, pulling her forward. Aware that she always had tasks saved for late-night hours on Christmas Eve, he placed a kiss on her cheek and let her go.

With one last look around at the happy crowd, she slipped out and headed for her room.

SEVENTEEN

Christmas morning arrived cloaked in heavy snow, a gray-white cocoon around the hotel, the kind that whispers *stay inside, stay warm, stay together... just stay.*

Mist rose before six, even after working into the early-morning hours to combine canvas and paint into tiny traveling memories. This was always her intention when creating miniature paintings for the guests. They weren't meant to be fancy or valuable or advertorial or anything other than a glimpse of a moment in time, whether one spent in Timberton or one reflected upon while there. No rules applied, and often Mist had no idea what her brushes would offer the small squares of canvas clipped to her easel. But something always appeared once she raised her hand, brush ready, in the air. So it had been the night before, and those now waited within the tree's branches, wrapped in silk fabric remnants, tied with natural raffia ribbon.

Clive was the first to pass through the lobby, having always had an uncanny knack for knowing when a pot of coffee was ready. He filled a mug with the fresh brew and took it into the front room, where he busied himself building a fire while Mist met up with Betty in the kitchen.

As complex as Christmas Eve dinner tended to be—especially this year—breakfast and brunch on Christmas Day were the opposite. For one thing, it was the only morning that the café was not open to locals. The only customers were overnight guests of the hotel. For another, most found themselves still recovering from the lavish meal the night before, and they preferred varying degrees of light and simple fare.

Thus, with the much smaller group in mind, Mist had made a cinnamon french toast casserole in advance. Clive would be in charge of any egg requests, offering guests the exotic options of either scrambled or fried. A platter of fresh melon slices and berries complimented the rest of the meal, and a beverage bar of chilled juices added to the warmer options of coffee, tea, or hot chocolate. It was simple, and it was just right.

Not surprisingly, the youngest guest was the first to appear. Serena tiptoed down the stairs, so focused on her quest that she didn't notice Mist setting a pitcher of creamer beside the coffee in the lobby.

"Good morning, magical elf," Mist said. "Merry Christmas."

"I'm not a magical elf today." Serena, dressed in red plaid pajamas, stood on the bottom step of the staircase and craned her neck to see the Christmas tree in the front parlor.

"I see," Mist said. "Well, I think you'll always be a magical elf." She did a quick inventory of tea selections and brought a few more out from behind the registration counter.

"Oh, look!" Serena skipped into the parlor and crouched down in front of the tree. "More presents!"

"Yes, I did see a few that weren't there last night." Mist smiled. Aside from those she had placed herself, guests had managed to sneak gifts under the tree when unsuspecting recipients weren't looking.

"I'm going to tell Mom to wake up."

Serena zipped back up the stairs, and Valerie passed her on the way down. She stifled a yawn, gladly accepting an offer of what Mist referred to as "java love."

"Thank you. There's nothing like the first sip of coffee in the morning!" Valerie cupped her hands around the hot mug, breathed in the fresh brew, and took a sip. "Fantastic!"

Rebecca and Tim soon followed, as did Clara and Andrew. As each guest joined the rest, they split into different areas, some lured by the warmth of the fire in the front room, others by the enticing aroma of cinnamon french toast in the café. Serena reappeared, Veronica in tow. The professor sought out his morning tea, which he enjoyed at a café table with Clara and Andrew. Michael took his regular chair by the fireplace after Mist insisted he should relax and enjoy the morning with the other guests.

"It feels very much like a family Christmas this year," Betty said when she and Mist had a moment alone in the kitchen. "It always does, of course, but this year feels especially so."

"I think you're right," Mist said, hearing the comfortable laughter and conversation coming from the front room.

"I can't pinpoint a reason though," Betty mused as she placed an empty casserole dish in the sink to soak.

Mist smiled. "Perhaps there isn't one. Perhaps it just is."

"Maybe so," Betty said. "Each year is a little different."

"And each year is a little wonderful." Mist thought over her statement and clarified it. "A *lot* wonderful."

"Valerie told me she plans to send a donation to the potbellied pig rescue when she sends the decorations for the beach cabin," Betty said.

Mist nodded. "I know Michael and Nigel are talking about a trip to the Gila Cliff Dwellings over spring break. They've already discussed it with Tim and Rebecca."

"Wonderful," Betty said as a burst of laughter reached the kitchen. "I'm going to see who might need a refill of coffee or tea."

"I'll be right behind you."

Mist collected several plates from tables in the café and carried them into the kitchen. She stacked them on the counter to be washed after the morning activity wound down. With heavy snow continuing to fall, guests were more likely to stay inside than to go out, as often happened on Christmas afternoons. She'd keep the buffet stocked with fruit and muffins, and she'd make a point of having decks of cards and board games out where guests could find them.

Joining the others in the front room again, she was pleased to see guests had started exchanging personal gifts with each other. Andrew gave Clara a kiss as thanks for new work gloves, and Rebecca dangled a silver pendant in front of her that Tim had picked out at Clive's gallery. Multiple gifts formed a circle around Serena as she sat on the floor—new pajamas, books, a jewelry box—that Santa had the foresight to ship ahead of time. Veronica, seated on a chair just behind her, held a handmade card that Serena had made the day before with art supplies Mist had given her. It had been a covert project that Veronica had been forbidden to infiltrate.

Mist stood beside the Christmas tree, almost blending in with the pine branches in the green rayon dress she'd chosen for the morning. Once the remaining gifts had been opened, she removed the first of the silk-wrapped paintings from within the trees branches.

"It has become a Timberton Hotel tradition now to give each guest something to take home as a remembrance of your stay here. These are your gifts this year." Mist handed the first one to Serena, who wasted no time pulling the raffia and silk off to reveal the miniature painting.

"It's a magical elf!" Serena exclaimed. "It even has my striped Santa hat! It's... it's me!"

"Hold it up so we can see it," Clara said. Serena did as suggested, and murmurs of approval circled the room.

"I do believe it looks like you," the professor said, nodding with approval.

Clara and Andrew received the next gift, and both smiled when the silk covering slipped away and revealed their painting.

"The stable from the Living Nativity scene at the festival!" Clara held the painting up for all to see. "This will remind us of those darling children." She looked at Andrew. "We'll hang it with the others. It will become a part of our Mist quilt."

"You have a Mist quilt?" Valerie mused. "Oh, yes! I understand. You come here every year, don't you?"

Clara nodded. "We do. And each year we add a miniature painting next to the others. One square at a time, it's forming a quilt on the wall."

"A brilliant idea!" The professor said. "Perhaps I'll do that with mine."

"You don't have to hang them on the wall," Mist explained to the first-time guests. "They can sit on a shelf or on a tabletop." She reached into the tree and pulled out another square of silk and raffia, handing it to Valerie, who opened it and smiled before holding it up.

"What is it?" Serena looked at the image of swirling musical notes with odds and ends—a sprig of pine, an open book, a seashell, an apple—trying to make sense of the picture.

"It's the music in a room," Valerie said.

"What room?" Serena pressed.

"Any room," Valerie said. She mouthed a thank-you to Mist, who nodded and then gave Rebecca and Tim their gift, which they eagerly opened.

"A snowman! How lovely." Rebecca beamed.

"Not just any snowman." Tim pointed to the snowman's nose, slightly crooked.

"You're right! It's our snowman, the first one we ever built."

"It won't melt," Serena said. "Because it's a painting." Veronica smiled at her daughter's observation. She reached down and ruffled the child's hair affectionately.

"Professor," Mist said, handing him a gift, which was quickly opened.

"The chess board, how perfect." The professor held it up.

"That's so you can practice for next year," Andrew pointed out playfully, having won the highly anticipated game the night before.

The professor harrumphed. "You needn't remind me." He looked at Mist. "It's fantastic."

"Michael didn't get one yet," Serena pointed out.

"Well, Michael isn't really a guest anymore...," Mist said, a sly smile crossing her face.

"Yep," Clive said. "We can't seem to get rid of the guy now."

"But I do have one for him." Mist handed him a silk-and-raffia gift, just as she had the others. He opened it, pondered it momentarily, and then smiled as he held it up.

"There's nothing on it," Serena said, confused by the blank canvas.

"Because it's the future," Mist explained. She stepped behind Michael's chair and, in a gesture that was growing familiar, placed a hand on his shoulders. "We have yet to create it."

"I love it," Michael said. He reached up to squeeze her hand.

"What about Mom?" Serena asked.

113

"Well, I do have something for your mother." Mist circled back around to the Christmas tree. Instead of reaching into the branches for a small silk package, she retrieved a larger box from below, which she handed to a very puzzled Veronica.

"Open it, Mom!" Serena said.

Veronica untied a wide, wire-edged ribbon that held the box closed and removed the lid from the box. Looking inside, she gasped, her eyes filling with tears.

"What's wrong?" Serena asked, echoing the thoughts of others in the room.

"Absolutely nothing," Veronica said as she reached inside and lifted out a miniature painting of a pig. She held it out for others to see.

"It's Biscuit!" Serena shouted. She took the canvas from her mother and placed a kiss on the pig's snout.

"Good thing the paint is dry already." Clive chuckled.

"You may need to keep that one," Mist said. "But the rest are for your gift shop."

"Oh, our visitors will love these!" Veronica exclaimed. "They'll certainly sell."

"I hope those will help with the supplies you need to take care of the pigs you rescue," Mist said. "I'll send more after the holidays are over. I think we can sell a few in our gallery here, too, and forward those proceeds to you." Mist looked at Clive with a mischievous smile, which caused him to laugh.

"Of course!" Clive said, shrugging his shoulders. "What kind of gallery owner would I be if I didn't sell miniature paintings of pigs?"

"Exactly!" Betty laughed.

"A lovely Christmas morning," Rebecca said. Others echoed her sentiments.

"It's stormy outside," Mist said, looking out the window, "and expected to stay the same most of the day."

"Indeed quite blustery," the professor said.

"I'll keep the buffet in the café stocked, adding soup and sandwiches around noon," Mist continued. "Please help yourselves to card decks and board games if you'd like. And, as you can see, there are plenty of books right here." She gestured toward a tall bookcase to the right of the fireplace. "Enjoy your holiday home."

Mist retreated into the lobby, turning back to watch as guests stood and stretched, some gathering up gifts, others starting up conversations with each other. Andrew motioned to the chess table, reminding Michael that he'd agreed to play the winner of the previous night's game. Betty and Clive joined others by the fireplace to enjoy the warmth of the flames. All appeared content with Christmas morning, exactly as Mist had hoped. Satisfied, she returned to the kitchen and fixed herself a cup of peppermint tea, which she quietly sipped at the center counter, alone and very much at peace.

EIGHTEEN

"It always goes by so quickly," Betty said. "It's hard to believe the last guests have gone."

"Yes, it is," Mist said. "As if they arrived and departed within the same moment."

Mist and Betty stood on the front porch, cape and coat draped over their respective shoulders. Bright sunlight reflected off white snowdrifts left the day before.

"Even Michael and the professor have gone," Betty said. "I'd thought they might linger a day or two."

"They're cochairing a literary conference tomorrow at the university," Mist said before breaking into a smile. "But they'll be back."

"Well, certainly Michael will," Betty said teasingly.

"I imagine you're right." Mist laughed. "And I'm glad."

"Of course you are. I noticed you didn't exchange gifts this year."

"We decided not to," Mist said. "At least not this year. Like Clara and Andrew have said in the past, we are each other's gifts."

The two women remained quiet, reflecting on the past few days of laughter, shared stories, new friendships, culinary fare, and a town festival on top of it all. Finally Betty spoke up.

"It was so sweet of Valerie to give us those hand-painted silk scarves before she left. I love the starfish design on mine, and the turtles on yours are adorable. She's so talented."

"Yes, she is," Mist agreed.

"And can you believe the guests bought all those paintings you gave Veronica?"

Mist smiled. "Yes, that warmed my heart to see they wanted to contribute to the farm's rescue endeavors. I'll need to make more quickly to ship to the gift shop."

"Well, after hearing Serena talk about Biscuit so much, I think they wanted a pig of their own to take home."

"You could be right," Mist said. "Biscuit seems to be quite popular. I was rather taken by him myself. In fact…"

Betty laughed. "You didn't."

"Oh, yes I did," Mist said. "It's hanging on the wall near the window in my room." She looked at Betty. "Am I not allowed to paint a picture for myself?"

"Of course you are!" Betty exclaimed. "And I'm glad you did. We all need remembrances, and indeed each of these Christmas seasons offers something to remember. Speaking of which, I told Clive I'd stop by the gallery to see how his day-after-Christmas sales are going." She pulled a pair of mittens from her coat pocket and put them on. "Care to join me?"

"Not this time. You go on."

Mist watched as Betty made her way carefully down the front steps and along the icy sidewalk.

When the sweet hotelkeeper was out of sight, she stepped inside and closed the door. The silence of the hotel was a stark contrast to the music and laughter of recent days. But it was not unwelcome. There would be other days filled with holiday cheer in the future, and she would wait for them to arrive.

For now, all was as it should be. The new year was just around the corner, and she had pigs to paint.

BETTY'S COOKIE EXCHANGE RECIPES

Glazed Cinnamon Nuts
Yuletide Coconut Cherry Cookies
Candy Bar Pretzel Cookies
Chocolate Coconut Almond Cookies
Mary's Sugar Cookies
Chocolate Crinkle Cookies
Applesauce Cookies
Chocolate-Dipped Shortbread
Ethyl's Chocolate Fudge
Sugar Cakes
Buttercream Candy
Mom's Chocolate Nut Caramels
Black Walnut Cookies
Sunflower Refrigerator Cookies
Pretzel Chocolate Bites
Ethyl's Oatmeal Raisin Cookies
Goldbricks
Lemon-Blueberry Scones
Chocolate Sandwich Cheesecake Cookies
Peanut Butter Muffins
Snowballs
Rudolph's Oatmeal Cookies

GLAZED CINNAMON NUTS
(A family recipe)

Ingredients:

1 cup sugar
1/4 cup water
1/8 teaspoon cream of tartar
Heaping teaspoon of cinnamon
1 tablespoon butter
1 1/2 cups walnut halves

Directions:

Boil sugar, water, cream of tartar and cinnamon to soft ball stage (236 degrees.)

Remove from heat.

Add butter and walnuts.

Stir until walnuts separate.

Place on wax paper to cool.

YULETIDE COCONUT CHERRY COOKIES
(Submitted by Kim Davis, from her blog,
Cinnamon and Sugar and a Little Bit of Murder)

Snowy-white coconut and glistening red cherries add holiday cheer to these shortbread-style cookies, making them an ideal addition to Christmas cookie platters.

Makes 18–20 cookies.

Ingredients:

1/2 cup room temperature unsalted butter (substitute vegan margarine if desired, to make suitable for vegans)
1/2 cup granulated sugar
1/4 teaspoon almond extract
1-1/3 cups all-purpose flour
1 teaspoon baking powder
1/2 teaspoon salt (if using margarine, omit)
1 cup sweetened coconut flakes
20 small maraschino cherries, divided

Directions:

Drain the maraschino cherries. Cut 10 of the cherries in half, pat dry and set aside. Coarsely chop the remaining cherries, blot excess liquid, and set aside.

Cream together the butter (or margarine), sugar, and almond extract, for 2 minutes.

Whisk together the flour, baking powder, and salt, then stir into the butter mixture until incorporated.

Gently fold the reserved coarsely chopped cherries into the cookie dough.

Cover dough with plastic wrap and refrigerate 1 hour.

Preheat oven to 350 degrees (F).

Shape dough into walnut-sized balls. Roll in coconut flakes and place on parchment-lined baking sheets, leaving 2 inches between cookies.

Bake 10–12 minutes until bottom of cookies are slightly golden. Remove from oven and immediately press the reserved cherry halves into the center of each cookie.

Cool on cookie sheet for 5 minutes, then remove and cool completely on a wire rack.

CANDY BAR PRETZEL COOKIES

(Submitted by Kay Garrett)
Serves: Yield: 36 (3) inch cookies (yield may vary)

Ingredients:

2 cups all-purpose flour
1 tsp baking powder
½ tsp baking soda
1 tsp salt
1 cup butter, softened
1 cup light brown sugar
1 cup granulated sugar
⅔ cup smooth peanut butter
2 tsp pure vanilla extract
2 large eggs
1 [11] oz bag Snickers bars or Baby Ruth bars, cubed
1 cup chopped pretzels
1 cup cocktail peanuts, roughly chopped
1 cup milk-chocolate chips

Directions:

Preheat the oven to 350°F. Line 2 baking sheets with parchment paper.

Sift together the all-purpose flour, baking powder, baking soda, and salt. Set aside.

In the bowl of a stand mixer, cream together the softened butter, light brown sugar, granulated sugar, peanut butter, and vanilla. Beat for 3 minutes until smooth, fluffy, and light beige in color. Add the eggs one at a time, beating well after each addition. Stop to scrape the bowl periodically so all the ingredients fully combine.

Add the dry ingredients gradually while beating on low speed, mixing well between each addition.

Repeat until all the dry ingredients have been added, stopping to scrape the sides of the bowl as needed.

After all the dry ingredients have been added, increase the speed of the mixer and beat for 1 minute.

Use a large nonstick spatula to mix the cubed Snickers bars, pretzels, peanuts, and chocolate chips into the batter by hand. The batter will be stiff. Mix until the ingredients are evenly distributed.

Use a 2- or 4-oz. ice-cream scoop to separate the dough, depending on the size you prefer. Place the dough rounds at least 3 inches apart on the baking sheet to allow room to spread. Press the centers to flatten slightly for even baking.

Bake for 18 minutes, rotating the pans if needed, until golden. Cool on the cookie sheet for 5 minutes, then remove to a cooling rack to cool completely.

Chocolate Almond Coconut Cookies
(Submitted by Kay Garrett)

Ingredients:

1 cup butter
1 1/2 cups white sugar
1 1/2 cups brown sugar
4 eggs
3 teaspoons vanilla
4 1/2 cups flour
2 teaspoons baking soda
1 teaspoon salt
5 cups chocolate chips
2 cups sweetened coconut
2 cups chopped almonds

Directions:

Preheat oven to 375°F. Lightly grease cookie sheets.

Combine dry ingredients, set aside.

In a large bowl, cream the butter and sugars together. Beat in the eggs, one at a time, stir in the vanilla. Stir in the dry ingredients until well mixed, then stir in the chocolate chips, coconut, and almonds. Drop by rounded full tablespoons onto the prepared cookie sheets.

Bake for 8 to 10 minutes. Cool on baking sheet for 5 minutes before removing to a wire rack to cool completely.

MARY'S SUGAR COOKIES
(Submitted by Pat Davis)

Ingredients:

1 cup granulated sugar
1 cup powdered sugar
1 cup softened butter
2 eggs
1 cup veg oil
2 tsp vanilla
4 cups flour
1 tsp baking soda
1 tsp salt
1 tsp cream of tarter

Directions:

Cream together sugars, butter, and eggs.

Add vegetable oil and vanilla.

Mix together flour, baking soda, salt, and cream of tartar. Add to the other ingredients and mix until well-blended.

Separate into 2 parts, wrap in plastic wrap, and refrigerate overnight.

Take out 1 part at a time and roll in teaspoon-sized balls, roll in sugar, crisscross top with a fork.

Bake @ 350°F for approx. 6 minutes.

Makes about 100 cookies.

Chocolate Crinkle Cookies
(Submitted by Alisha Collins)

Ingredients:

1/2 cup (2.2 oz/60 g) unsweetened cocoa powder
1 cup (7 oz/205 g) white granulated sugar
1/4 cup (60ml) vegetable oil
2 large eggs
2 teaspoons pure vanilla extract
1 cup (3.5oz/130g) all purpose or plain flour
1 teaspoon baking powder
1/2 teaspoon salt
1/4 cup confectioners' sugar or icing sugar (for coating)

Directions:

In a medium-sized bowl, mix together the cocoa powder, white sugar, and vegetable oil. Beat in eggs one at a time until fully incorporated. Mix in the vanilla.
In another bowl, combine the flour, baking powder, and salt. Stir the dry ingredients into the wet mixture just until a dough forms (do not overbeat). Cover bowl with wrap and refrigerate for at least 4 hours or overnight.

When ready to bake, preheat oven to 350°F | 175°C. Line 2 cookie sheets or baking trays with parchment paper (baking paper). Roll 1 tablespoonful of dough into balls for smaller cookies, or 2 tablespoonfuls for larger cookies.

Add the confectioners' (icing) sugar to a smaller bowl. Generously and evenly coat each ball of dough in confectioners' sugar and place onto prepared cookie sheets.
Bake in preheated oven for 10 minutes (for small cookies) or 12 minutes (for larger cookies). The cookies will come out soft from the oven but will harden up as they cool.
Allow to cool on the cookie sheet for 5 minutes before transferring to wire racks to cool.

APPLESAUCE COOKIES

(Submitted by Valerie Peterson)

Ingredients:

½ cup butter
½ cup brown sugar
½ cup sugar
1 egg
1 teaspoon baking soda
1 cup applesauce
2 cups flour
½ teaspoon cloves
½ teaspoon salt
½ teaspoon cinnamon
1 teaspoon nutmeg

Directions:

Cream margarine, sugars, and eggs.

Add baking soda and applesauce.

Add dry ingredients.

Drop by teaspoon on greased cookie sheet.

Bake 8-10 minutes at 425 degrees.

CHOCOLATE-DIPPED SHORTBREAD
(Submitted by Alisha Collins)

Ingredients:

1 cup salted butter, cold and cut up into pieces
2/3 cup granulated sugar
1 teaspoon almond extract (if you'd prefer the nut taste to be milder, use vanilla extract)
½ cup pecan pieces (I put mine in the food processor to get them nice and small)
2 ¼ cups all-purpose flour
½ cup Nutella
¼ cup semisweet chocolate chips
2 tablespoons milk
1 tablespoon confectioners' sugar

Directions:

In the bowl of an electric mixer, cream butter and sugar. Add in almond (or vanilla) extract. When these ingredients are well blended, add pecan pieces.

Gradually add flour and mix at low speed until combined, then increase speed to medium until your dough is no longer sandy-looking.

Put a piece of parchment paper on a baking tray, and turn dough out of mixing bowl. Divide in half. Form each half into a rectangle. I use my thumb as a width guide. Cover with plastic wrap and chill for 1 hour.

Preheat oven to 350 degrees.

Unwrap dough and use a pizza cutter to cut into sticks. Keep sticks close together on tray so they don't spread.

Bake in preheated oven for 15-20 minutes or until shortbread is golden and semifirm to the touch,

Cool completely.

Over a double boiler, melt the semisweet chocolate chips, milk, sugar, and Nutella until smooth. You can also use a glass bowl in the microwave. Just make sure the chocolate doesn't burn.

Dip your shortbread sticks into the chocolate-Nutella mixture. Let cookies harden on parchment paper or just gobble them up there and then.

ETHYL'S CHOCOLATE FUDGE
(Submitted by Erica Younce)

Ingredients:

4 cups sugar
1 cup milk
½ cup cocoa
1 cup evaporated milk
3 tablespoons butter
1 teaspoon vanilla

Directions:

Mix sugar, cocoa, and milk; mix well, then add evaporated milk.

Boil until mixture is set when dropped into cold water.

Add butter and vanilla.

Sit cooker down in a sink of cold water and beat until it starts getting thick.

Pour into 9" square pan. Cut into squares. Enjoy!

SUGAR CAKES
(Submitted by Penny Lee Barton)

Ingredients:

½ lb. butter
2 cups sugar
3 eggs
1 tablespoon vanilla or lemon extract
4 cups flour
2 teaspoons baking powder
1 cup sour milk (1 cup milk + 1 tablespoon vinegar)
1 ½ teaspoons baking soda
½ teaspoon cream of tartar

Directions:

Mix all liquid ingredients except milk.

Mix milk and vinegar and set aside for 5 minutes.

Add dry ingredients, then add sour milk. Mix well.

Drop by teaspoon on greased cookie sheet.

Bake at 350 degrees for 10 minutes.

BUTTERCREAM CANDY

(Submitted by Colleen Galster)

Ingredients:

1 lb. 10x sugar
¼ lb. butter
1 tablespoon evaporated milk
1 teaspoon vanilla
Pinch of salt
Semisweet chocolate chips

Directions:

Mix all ingredients (except the chocolate chips) until it no longer sticks to your hands. If it does, add a little more 10x sugar until it no longer sticks.

Form into balls or whatever shape you choose, then place on a tray. Refrigerate for at least an hour until the buttercream is hardened some.

Melt the chocolate and coat the buttercream. Place back in the refrigerator until ready to serve. Keep refrigerated is best.

MOM'S CHOCOLATE NUT CARAMELS
(Submitted by Lanette Fields)

Ingredients:

1 (15 Oz) can sweetened condensed milk
1 cup light corn syrup
1 tablespoon butter
1/8 teaspoon salt
2 squares unsweetened chocolate
1 teaspoon vanilla extract
2/3 cup finely chopped nuts

Directions:

In a heavy 1 ½ quart saucepan, mix 1/3 cup of milk with corn syrup, butter, and salt.

Cook over medium heat, stirring constantly, until candy thermometer reaches 235 degrees.

Slowly stir in remaining milk, keeping mixture boiling.

Add chocolate one square at a time and continue cooking until temperature reaches 235 again.

Remove from heat and stir in vanilla.

Sprinkle half of the chopped nuts into a buttered 8" square pan.

Pour in caramel mixture and sprinkle with remaining chopped nuts. Cool completely.

Cut into squares using buttered kitchen scissors. Makes one pound.

BLACK WALNUT COOKIES
(Submitted by Jeannie Daniel)

Ingredients:

1 cup butter, softened
2 cups packed brown sugar
2 eggs
1 tablespoon molasses
1 teaspoons vanilla
3 1/2 cups all-purpose flour
1 teaspoon baking soda
1/4 teaspoon salt
2 cups chopped black walnuts, divided

Directions:

Cream the butter and brown sugar together, beat in eggs and vanilla. Combine flour, baking soda, and salt.

Gradually add the dry ingredients to the egg mixture. Stir in 1 ¼ cup walnuts. Finely chop the remaining nuts.

Shape dough into two 15-inch-long logs.

Roll the logs in the chopped nuts, pressing gently. Wrap in plastic wrap or towel. Refrigerate for 2 hours.

Unwrap and cut into 1/4-inch slices. Place 2 inches apart on greased cookie sheets.

Bake at 300 degrees for 12 minutes. Cool. Makes about 10 dozen cookies.

Sunflower Refrigerator Cookies

(Submitted by Valerie Peterson)

Ingredients:

½ cup butter
½ cup brown sugar
1 teaspoon vanilla
¾ cup whole wheat flour
¼ cup wheat germ
¼ teaspoon salt
½ teaspoon baking soda
¾ cup dry-roasted sunflower seeds
½ cup sugar
1 egg
1 ½ cup quick oatmeal

Directions:

Cream butter and sugars. Add egg. Beat well.

Stir together dry ingredients, then add to creamed mixture.
Add sunflower seeds.

Divide dough into 2 rolls and wrap in wax paper. Chill at least
4 hours.

Cut into ¼ slices.

Bake at 375 degrees for 10–12 minutes or until lightly browned.

Pretzel Chocolate Bites
(Submitted by Cecile VanTyne)

Ingredients:

Mini pretzels
Rolo candy
Christmas M&M's

Directions:

Preheat the oven to 200 degrees.

On a cookie sheet, lay down as many pretzels as you'd like to make and put a Rolo on top of each one.

Bake for about 5 min until soft, remove from the oven, and put an M&M on each one.

Let them sit until they firm up and enjoy!

ETHYL'S OATMEAL RAISIN COOKIES
(Submitted by Bea Tackett)

Ingredients:

1 cup soft shortening
1 ½ cups sugar
2 eggs
½ cup buttermilk
1 ¾ cups flour
1 teaspoon baking soda
1 teaspoon baking powder
½ teaspoon salt
1 teaspoon cinnamon
2 cups rolled oats
1 cup raisins, cut up
½ cup raisins, chopped

Directions:

Mix thoroughly: shortening, sugar, and eggs.

Stir in buttermilk.

Sift together and stir in flour, baking soda, baking powder, salt, and cinnamon.

Stir in rolled oats, raisins, nuts.

Drop rounded teaspoons 2 inches apart on an ungreased baking sheet.

Bake at 400 degrees for 8–10 minutes or until lightly browned.

Makes 5 ½ doz.

Goldbricks

(Submitted by Jan Knight)

Ingredients:

1 angel food cake mix OR your favorite scratch recipe
1 recipe of your favorite vanilla buttercream OR store bought
Salted peanuts -fined chopped (either salted in the shell OR canned)

Directions:

Bake the angel food as directed in a large loaf pan (16-inches long x 4 1/2 inches wide x 4 inches high OR 2 regular 9 x 5 loaf pans.)

Bake as directed & let cool.

Cut the cake into small logs 4 by 1 1/2-inch square.

Frost on all sides & roll in finely chopped peanuts (easier with 2 people - one to frost, one to roll in nuts).

Store in cool place or refrigerator with wax paper between layers OR freeze.

These actually get better with age!

LEMON BLUEBERRY SCONES
(Submitted by Shelia Hall)

Ingredients:

2 cups (250g) all-purpose flour (spoon & leveled), plus more for hands and work surface
6 tablespoons (75g) granulated sugar
1 tablespoon fresh lemon zest (about 1 lemon)
2 and 1/2 teaspoons baking powder
1/2 teaspoon salt
1/2 cup (1 stick; 115g) unsalted butter, frozen
1/2 cup (120ml) heavy cream (plus 2 Tbsp for brushing)
1 large egg
1 and 1/2 teaspoons pure vanilla extract
1 heaping cup (180g) fresh or frozen blueberries (do not thaw)
for topping: coarse sugar

Lemon Icing

1 cup (120g) confectioners' sugar
3 tablespoons fresh lemon juice (about 1 large lemon)

Directions:

Whisk flour, sugar, lemon zest, baking powder, and salt together in a large bowl. Grate the frozen butter using a box grater. Add it to the flour mixture and combine with a pastry cutter, two forks, or your fingers until the mixture comes together in pea-sized crumbs. Place in the refrigerator or freezer as you mix the wet ingredients together.

Whisk 1/2 cup heavy cream, the egg, and vanilla extract together in a small bowl. Drizzle over the flour mixture, add the blueberries, then mix together until everything appears moistened.

Pour onto the counter and, with floured hands, work dough into a ball as best you can. Dough will be sticky. If it's too sticky, add a little more flour. If it seems too dry, add 1 or 2 more tablespoons heavy cream. Press into an 8-inch disk and, with a sharp knife or bench scraper, cut into 8 wedges.

Brush scones with remaining heavy cream, and for extra crunch, sprinkle with coarse sugar. (You can do this before or after refrigerating in the next step.)

Place scones on a plate or lined baking sheet (if your fridge has space!) and refrigerate for at least 15 minutes.

Meanwhile, preheat oven to 400°F (204°C).

Line a large baking sheet with parchment paper or silicone baking mat. After refrigerating, arrange scones 2 to 3 inches apart on the prepared baking sheet(s).

Bake for 22–25 minutes or until golden brown around the edges and lightly browned on top.

Remove from the oven and cool for a few minutes before topping with lemon icing.

Make the icing: Whisk the icing ingredients together. Drizzle over warm scones.

Leftover iced or un-iced scones keep well at room temperature for 2 days or in the refrigerator for 5 days.

CHOCOLATE SANDWICH CHEESECAKE COOKIES
(Submitted by Shelia Hall)

Ingredients:

1 8-ounce package cream cheese, softened
2 sticks butter, softened
1½ cups sugar
2 cups flour
20 chocolate sandwich cookies, coarsely chopped

Directions:

In a large bowl, beat cream cheese, butter, and sugar using a hand mixer or stand mixer until well blended. This should take a couple of minutes. You could use a whisk to do this by hand, just expect an intense arm workout.

Slowly add flour and mix until fully incorporated. Gently fold in cookies.

Cover your bowl with plastic wrap and chill the cookie dough in the fridge for at least 30 minutes. Chilling the dough is key here! The fat in the dough needs to solidify a bit to hold their shape while baking.

When you're ready to bake, preheat your oven to 350°F. On a cookie sheet lined with parchment paper, roll dough into balls using a cookie scoop (or 2 Tbsp. per cookie). Gently press the dough down with the back of a spoon to make a cookie shape. Tip: spray the spoon with nonstick spray first to prevent sticking.

Bake 12–15 minutes or until the edges are lightly brown and the center is puffed up.

Let them cool on the pan for 5 minutes before cooling completely on a wire rack.

PEANUT BUTTER MUFFINS
(Submitted by Jennifer Schmidt)

Ingredients:

1 bag Reese's miniature peanut butter cups
½ cup margarine
½ cup brown sugar
½ cup sugar
1 egg
1 teaspoon vanilla
½ cup creamy peanut butter
1 ½ cups flour
¾ teaspoon baking soda

Directions:

Spray or grease mini muffin pans or use mini cupcake papers.

Roll dough into small balls and place into muffin tins.

Bale for 8–9 minutes at 375 degrees.

Remove from oven; immediately put a peanut butter cup in the middle of each and push down.

Let cool.

SNOWBALLS

(Submitted by Petrenia Etheridge)

Ingredients:

1 stick salted butter, softened
1/2 cup brown sugar
1 cup all-purpose flour
1 teaspoon ground cinnamon
1 teaspoon vanilla
1/2 cup finely chopped walnuts
Confectioners' sugar for rolling

Directions:

Cream butter, sugar, and cinnamon.

Add in flour and vanilla, mix well.

Stir in walnuts and a tablespoon of water, if necessary.

Use a teaspoon-size amount and roll into balls.

Place on greased cookie sheet or parchment paper.

Bake at 300 degrees for approx. 25 min.

Let cool to slightly warm and roll in confectioners' sugar.

Roll a second time if desired to make them nice and snowy.

RUDOLPH'S OATMEAL COOKIES
(Submitted by Brenda Ellis)

Ingredients:

1 cup butter, room temperature
1 cup brown sugar
1/2 cup granulated sugar
2 eggs
1 teaspoon vanilla
1 1/2 cups all-purpose flour
1 teaspoon baking soda

1 teaspoon cinnamon
1/2 tsp salt
3 cups old-fashioned oats
1 cup fresh cranberries, quartered
1 cup pecans, chopped
1 cup white chocolate chips

Directions:

Preheat oven to 350 degrees.

Cream together butter and sugars until creamy.

Mix in eggs one at a time, then mix in vanilla.

In a separate bowl, whisk together flour, baking soda, cinnamon, and salt.

Add the flour mixture to the butter/sugar mixture and mix well.

Stir in oats, cranberries, pecans, and white-chocolate chips.

Drop about 1 tablespoon of dough on cookie sheet, leaving 2 inches between.

Bake 10–12 minutes or until edges start to brown.

Cool on a cooling rack.

ACKNOWLEDGMENTS

Christmas in the small town of Timberton is always joyful, thanks to resident artist and chef, Mist. But much of this is due to the creative efforts of others. I'm grateful to Annie Sarac at The Editing Pen, whose editing expertise catches every wayward comma and polishes manuscripts into the spiffiest shape possible. Elizabeth Christy is also owed thanks for assisting with plot development as well as nudging me forward with constant words of encouragement. As with other covers in the Moonglow Christmas series, credit for the Yuletide at Moonglow design goes to Keri Knutson of Alchemy Book Covers. Jay Garner and Karen Putnam always deserve a round of applause for their top-notch beta reading and feedback.

Betty's annual cookie exchange not only fills the Timberton Hotel with the sweet smell of baked goods, but allows readers to contribute and share favorite recipes. Heartfelt thanks go to Kim Davis and her blog, Cinnamon and Sugar and a Little Bit of Murder, Kay Garrett, Penny Lee Barton, Pat Davis, Lanette Fields, Shelia Hall, Alisha Collins, Petrenia Etheridge, Erica Younce, Jennifer Schmidt, Bea Tackett, Valerie Peterson, Jan Knight, Colleen Galster, Jeannie Daniel, Cecile VanTyne and Brenda Ellis for providing recipes for this year's delicious goodies. Enjoy!

RECIPE NOTES

RECIPE NOTES

RECIPE NOTES

RECIPE NOTES

RECIPE NOTES

RECIPE NOTES

CPSIA information can be obtained
at www.ICGtesting.com
Printed in the USA
LVHW110249021220
673195LV00006B/110